Critical Acclaim for AVA

"AVA, Carole Maso's third novel, is that rare event, a formal literary experiment that is also compelling as a work of fiction. Maso is a writer of such power and originality that the reader is carried with her far beyond the usual limits of the novel. . . . Maso's voice is all her own: simultaneously cerebral and sensual, violently romantic and insistently woman-centered." —*San Francisco Chronicle* (front page)

"Poetic, rapturous. . . . Like a piece of music, AVA uses repetition and thematic layering to create a shimmering, impressionistic portrait that eschews linear narrative in favor of the sensations aroused by resonant imagery." —*New York Times Book Review*

"Give Carole Maso and her publisher an A for audacity. . . . [AVA] reads like poetry." —*Los Angeles Times Book Review*

"Lovely . . . the product of a rigorous and imaginative formal intelligence." —*Voice Literary Supplement*

"What [Virginia Woolf] did for the prose rhythm of the paragraph, Maso has done for the sentence. . . . [AVA] is to be read slowly, with great pleasure." —*Chicago Tribune*

"Presents heartbreakingly familiar emotions in an utterly original form." —*Publishers Weekly* (starred review)

"Richly textured. . . . Maso has written another spellbinder." —*Library Journal* (starred review)

"AVA . . . is a key to understanding this deeply important writer." —*L.A. Weekly*

"Maso's third novel is a moving, symphonic testimony to the meanings that memory, desire, and life accumulate. . . . An erotic and moving book, AVA reconfirms Maso's reputation as one of our most refined and daring novelists." —*Booklist*

"A mysterious and richly allusive novel. . . . In her description of the evocative details of physical life, Maso contributes new insights into women's inner life." —*Choice*

"AVA is unique in its blend of prose, poetry, critical theory, and narrative. Maso has created a collage that further blurs the distinctions between fiction and poetry and between the modern and the postmodern. Like Pound, she sets ideas and images against one another without drawing narrative connections, encouraging the reader to act as equal particpant in constructing images, characters, scenes from Ava's life, and theory from music, literature, and the visual arts." —*American Book Review*

"Maso challenges contemporary fiction in a way in which very few young American novelists are capable. In AVA she has dismantled the traditional linear narrative while a story persists. She steps through the experimentation of some of the great writers of modernism into the company of some of the brilliant innovators among her contemporaries." —*Central Park*

"Ava's story is an extraordinary love letter spun into gold." —*Columbus Dispatch*

"For so innovative a novel, AVA proves wonderfully readable: unconventional yet accessible, as sensuous as it is cerebral, appealing, even inviting, allusive but never aloof, at times unbearably sad." —*Magill Book Reviews*

AVA

ALSO BY CAROLE MASO

Ghost Dance

The Art Lover

The American Woman in the Chinese Hat

AVA

A NOVEL BY

Carole Maso

DALKEY ARCHIVE PRESS

© 1993 by Carole Maso
First published in hardcover by Dalkey Archive Press, 1993
First paperback edition, 1995

Library of Congress Cataloging-in-Publication Data
Maso, Carole.
   Ava : a novel / by Carole Maso.
   I. Title.
PS3563.A786A95   1993   92-35600
813'.54—dc20

ISBN 1-56478-074-0

Partially funded by grants from the National Endowment for the Arts and
the Illinois Arts Council.

NATIONAL
ENDOWMENT
FOR ❤ THE
A R T S

Dalkey Archive Press
Illinois State University
Campus Box 4241
Normal, IL 61790-4241

Printed on permanent/durable acid-free paper and bound in the United States of
America.

One thousand love letters

To Rosemarie, my mother, origin of all happiness, poetry, song.

To Judith and Zenka, who gave me France.

To Barbara, Dixie, Laura, and Angela, dear friends.

And as always, to Helen.

August 15

MORNING

Each holiday celebrated with real extravagance. Birthdays. Independence days. Saints' days. Even when we were poor. With verve.

Come sit in the morning garden for awhile.

Olives hang like earrings in late August.

A perpetual pageant.

A throbbing.

Come quickly.

The light in your eyes

Precious. Unexpected things.

Mardi Gras: a farewell to the flesh.

You spoke of Trieste. Of Constantinople. You pushed the curls from your face. We drank Five-Star Metaxa on the island of Crete and aspired to the state of music.

Olives hang like earrings.

A throbbing. A certain pulsing.

The villagers grew violets.

We ran through genêt and wild sage.

Labyrinth of Crete, mystery of water, home.

On this same street we practiced arias, sang sad songs, duets, received bitter news, laughed, wept.

Green, how much I want you green.

We ran through genêt and wild sage.

You are a wild one, Ava Klein.

We were working on an erotic song cycle.

He bounded up the sea-soaked steps.

She sang like an angel. Her breast rose and fell with each breath.

Night jasmine. Already?

On this slowly moving couchette.

Not yet.

Tell me everything that you want.

Wake up, Ava Klein. Turn over on your side. Your right arm, please.

Tell me everything you'd like me to—your hand there, slowly.

Pollo alla Diavola. A chicken opened flat. Marinated in olive oil, lemon juice. On a grill. A Roman specialty.

Up close you are like a statue.

After all the dolci—the nougat, candied oranges and lemon peel, ginger and burnt almonds, anisette—my sweet . . . after walnut biscotti and lovemaking, Alfred Hitchcock's Vertigo. . . . Francesco, what was conspiring against us, even then?

This same corner I now turn in bright light, in heat and in some fear, I once turned in snow and the mind calls that up reminded of—

The way you looked that night, on your knees.

Reminded of: a simple game of Hide and Seek. Afterwards a large fire.

Sundays are always so peaceful here.

A child in a tree.

August.

I dream of you and Louise and the giant poodle, Lily, and the beach.

But it is not of course that summer anymore.

August. They sit together on a lawn in New York State in last light—bent, but only slightly.

Come quickly, there are finches at the feeder.

Let me know if you are going.

The small village. I could not stay away. My two dear friends. Always there. Arms outstretched, waiting.

A dazzle of fish.

My hand reaching for a distant, undiscovered planet.

Through water.

Where we never really felt far from the sea.

He kept drawing ladders.

We dressed as the morning star and birds.

He bows his head in shadow. He turns gentle with one touch. In the Café Pourquoi Pas, in the Café de Rien, in the Café Tout Va Bien where we seemed to live then.

We were living a sort of café life.

Let me describe my life here.

You can't believe the fruit!

I'd like to imagine there was music.

Pains in the joints. Dizziness. Some pain.

A certain pulsing.

She's very pregnant.

I'd like to imagine there was music in the background.

And that you sang.

What is offhand, overheard. Bits of remembered things.

Morning. And the nurses, now. Good morning, Ava Klein.

Ava Klein, Francesco says, helping me on with my feather head-dress.

Brazil, 1988; Venice, 1976; Quebec, 1980.

Determined to reshape the world according to the dictates of desire—

Where we dressed as the planets and danced.

Spinning. To you—

Charmed, enchanted land.

Chinatown. A favorite Chinese restaurant. The way he held my hand. As if it were a polished stone. Steam and ginger. News that the actress you most wanted had agreed to the part and financing had come. On the street, rain, a yellow taxi cab. I love you.

[6]

He bounded up the sea-soaked steps.

Music moves in me. Shapes I've needed to complete. Listen, listen hard.

It's cool at this hour—morning. How is it that I am back here again, watering and watering the gardens?

And you are magically here somehow.

A heartbeat away.

We have a curious way, however, of being dependent on unexpected things, and among these are the unexpected transformations of

Poetry.

And he is here in front of me asking, Qu'est-ce que tu bois?

Blood and seawater have identical levels of potassium, calcium and magnesium.

Wild roses and rose hips.

The rose.

Qu'est-ce que tu bois?

Summer in New York. I'm thirsty.

I say "water" in my sleep. I'm thirsty. You bring me a tall glass of water and place it by my bed.

And one is reminded of: We were driving from New York City up the Saw Mill Parkway toward the Taconic and listening to the *Wanderer* Symphony of Schubert on the radio. I begged you to slow down, but as slowly as you drove, we were still losing it in the static, long before it finished.

You are a rare bird.

And I had to complete it in my head.

Which is different from hearing it completed on WNYC.

Though I sang it LOUD. All the parts.

It was completing itself, in midtown Manhattan without us.

Though I knew the ending and tried to sing it LOUD, without

You are beautiful

forgetting any of the important parts.

How is this for a beginning?

There is scarcely a day that goes by that I do not think of you.

Turn over on your side.

My heart is breaking.

New York in summer.

The Bleecker Street Cinema. Monica Vitti on the rocks.

Danilo laments the U.S.A. He says we have forgotten how to be Americans.

Maria Ex Communikata gets ready for the midnight show.

The Bleecker Street Cinema closes for good. And suddenly it is clear,

We are losing.

The scales tip.

Please invoice me. Input me. Format me. Impact me.

The bullet meant for Ricardo hits Renee instead. The bullet meant for target #1 hits baby Fawn. A bullet kills Daryl, honor student.

We will go to the river. We will rent a boat.

There were flowers each day in the market in Venice.

And how your hands trembled at a gift of exquisite yellow roses, so beautiful, and pas cher, Emma.

To hear you say japonica in your British accent once more.

Tell him that you saw us.

Because the corner of Broadway and West Houston is everyone's in summer.

I think of his life. That somewhere else it was completing itself. Somewhere outside my reach. Without me.

Though there was no way for me to know, unlike Schubert's *Wanderer*, how it was going to be played out.

Somewhere a young girl learns how to hold a pencil. She writes A.

To sing the endless variations on the themes he set up.

Thirty-five years old. Aldo.

Because the guandu, Ana Julia's favorite food, when we could finally bear to use it was no longer good. Expiration date: 1989.

I might turn the corner and there will be Cha-Cha Fernández walking a Doberman pinscher.

I can see it all from here.

Rare butterflies.

Nymphets by the pool.

Danilo, working out an unemployment scam for himself. Plotting a trip to Prague. Can you come?

The *Prague*, the *Paris*, the *Jupiter*, to name a few. Can you come?

I miss Czechoslovakia sometimes.

I'll probably never see you again.

Of course you will.

I might look up and there will be the Fuji Film blimp.

Or Samuel Beckett in a tree.

They are singing low in my ear, now. In the morning garden.

He grew old roses.

So what's the war about? someone asks. In brief.

Impact me. Impact me harder.

She finds herself on her thirty-third birthday on a foreign coast with a man named Carlos.

Never stop.

He is worried the city will get better—but not for a while, and not before it gets worse.

The man on the TV wants them to freeze his head while he is alive, and to attach his brain to another body sometime later, when they find the cure for his incurable brain tumor.

How are you Ava Klein?

What answer would you be interested in other than the truth?

Make a wish.

The blue and purple in your black hair, Carlos. . . .

Danilo is writing a love story where the beloved makes the mistake of not existing.

Ava Klein, you are a rare bird.

Because decidedly, I do not want to miss the grand opening scheduled for early winter, still some months away, of the new Caribbean restaurant down the block that will serve goat.

Or the cold.

Or the Beaujolais Nouveau.

And so: Monday: chemotherapy. Tuesday: reiki. Wednesday: acupuncture. Thursday: visualization. Friday: experimental potions, numbers one through twelve. Monday: chemotherapy.

This room. White curtains to the floor. Wide pine panels. Painted white. Like the room in a dream.

The iris, Marie-Claude, like you, so glowing and grave.

Thank you for the tiger lilies.

In an attempt between 1968 and 1970 to fashion a perfectly round sphere, he made three thousand balls of mud, all unsuccessful;

I wrote you fifty love letters.

She has lived to tell it. How to make the family challah: sugar, flour, oil, kosher salt, eggs, honey.

I ran through broom and wild sage.

We took the overnight train.

You are a wild one, Ava Klein.

The men hung swordfish in the trees to dry. Sword snouts. Teeth in the trees.

He spoke of Trieste, of Constantinople. He pushed the curls from his face, thought of buying a hat perhaps. My first honeymoon. It was how the days went.

The changing of the guard.

In Crete, a gold-toothed porter.

She sang like an angel. Her breast rose with each breath.

I needed to travel.

Aida sits in the day's first square of light.

I love your breasts.

It was Rome. I was twenty, and you were forty, almost. You were making a film of the *Inferno*. I laughed imagining the task. I was a graduate student. A student of comparative literature. I held your giant hand. You pressed me against a broken wall in the furnace called August. I kissed you. Or you kissed me.

Yes, but it is not that August anymore.

And in 1971 the artist carved 926 sculptures from sugar cubes.

That evening he led me into the circular room.

A woman named Yvette Poisson dancing in a glass bar in the seaside resort in winter.

A perfect gray sea. Grayness of the days.

Let me know if you are going—

Snow fell on water.

We took the overnight train. He kissed me everywhere. Shapely trees passing in the windows.

A beautiful landscape. Imagined in the dark.

The way his body swelled.

Trees that looked like other things.

He tries to conserve moments of existence by placing them in biscuit boxes.

At the feeder, goldfinches.

Danilo, my Czech novelist, with his deep mistrust of words. His fear of the Russians. His love of Nabokov.

And Flaubert is *not* Madame Bovary, students, I don't care what he says.

The Empire State Building is working overtime emoting in colored lights for every cause known to man: international children, the Irish, hostages, Fourth of July.

Václav Havel: Everywhere in the world, people were surprised how these malleable, humiliated, cynical citizens of Czechoslovakia, who seemingly believed in nothing, found the tremendous strength within a few weeks to cast off the totalitarian systems in an entirely peaceful and dignified manner. We ourselves are surprised at it.

Strange the way the joy keeps changing.

I remember the smell of rosemary and thyme in a young man's hair.

It was a kind of paradise, Anatole.

He makes a record on which he tries to remember the lullabies he might have heard as a child.

The morning nurse singing, Let me know if you are going to Central Park. Lunch break 12:30.

I hear water. You come around the rounded stone fountain. Ça va? I say. And you nod.

At La Fontaine des Quatre Dauphins in Aix, where I wept.

To see your beautiful head turn.

To see your beautiful head turn once more.

But we've already lost so much.

The heat of a plot. I'm beginning to detect the heat of the plot.

García Lorca feigning death.

Václav Havel comes to town. Danilo tries to meet him on this, his triumphant visit. Havel, being pushed out for five minutes at a time here, there to speak with American dignitaries. Also with Frank Langella, Paul Simon, Carly Simon, etc., John Irving in the corner. (Nobody wanted to talk to him.) This one, that one—poor Havel. Danilo looks pained.

It was as if we had come in on a conversation midway. That was the kind of beginning it was.

The late verses of Neruda vary widely in tone and texture. Their fluctuating musical impulses require a looser structure woven together less by the uniformity of lines than by the dying poet's sensibilities.

A stroll around the park. While the weather's still fine. The ginkgo trees in fall.

Un, deux, trois.

A simple game of Hide and Seek.

Danilo to his last, crazy lover: I'm going to take the garbage out. And she responds, What, you're going to see Gorbachev now? She shakes her head. Go then!

Turn over on your side.

[14]

And it will seem like music.

A blue like no other.

Maria Regina remembers the fascists: They told us to mount the stairs two at a time.

Often there is nowhere to go but forward or back. It is hard to stay here in one place and especially at moments like these.

I am afraid the news is bad, Ava Klein.

Now in America, they call this coffee. But I remember coffee. . . .

A simple game of Hide and Seek.

The giant head of Françoise Gilot in stone. We took photographs, though photographs were not allowed. Marie-Claude and Emma and Anatole and me, smiling in the bright light and so much sea, in the room called Joie de Vivre.

The Musée Picasso. Antibes.

He was on his way to see Gorbachev when we met for the first time on the street. It seems that all along we were neighbors.

Ten, eleven, twelve. . . .

I kiss you a thousand times.

Making mysterious La Joconde faces next to Françoise Gilot one afternoon.

Vladimir Nabokov: The book you sent me is one of the tritest and most tedious examples of a trite and tedious genre. The plot and those extravagant "deep" conversations affect me as bad as movies do, or the worst plays and stories of Leonid Andreyev, with whom Faulkner has a kind of fatal affinity. I imagine that this kind of thing (white trash, velvety Negroes, those bloodhounds out of Uncle Tom's Cabin melodramas, steadily baying through thousands of swampy books) may be necessary in a social sense, but it is not litera-ture. . . . (and especially those ghastly italics).

[15]

The emblem is for a group called Missing Foundation. An upside-down champagne glass with the champagne crossed out. The party's over is what the emblem stands for. And everything points to it—that the party is over.

Would you like to have a perfect memory?

Because there is still Verdi and sunlight and the memory of that man on the Riviera—and when memory goes it is replaced maybe with beautiful, floating, free, out of context fish. Orange in deep blue with tails like feathers.

Or Samuel Beckett learning to fly.

Vitello Tonato: Boneless veal roast, white wine, anchovies, capers, tuna, a sprig of thyme.

It's a hot and lovely day. No humidity—odd for this city. A clear sky, high clouds. And the weather is for everyone.

What's the rush then?

Unable to get to you, Marie-Claude and Emma, any other way right now, I dream of the fish in your stone pond. I send you a report of the weather.

We are making a day trip to Cap d'Antibes. How much we wish you were here!

Aldo recalls his grandfather: he is gnawing on the end of an anisette biscuit with the perfect pointy teeth he acquired right before his death.

INTERVIEWER: If you could remember only one thing, what would it be?

FRISCH: A landscape or a man-woman relationship.

INTERVIEWER: If you could have written only one book, which would it have been?

FRISCH: It should have been a very excellent one, but since I didn't succeed in that, I had to write many. Actually, my feelings about that change from time to time. I think it would not be theater but one of the narrative works. And if I'm still allowed to have a wish, I'd say none of the books but a poem.

INTERVIEWER: What is your greatest regret?

FRISCH [long pause]: Yes, but of course, not to be wise, not to be as wise as I pretend to be. That I'm not a little bit more serious— yes, I would say that's it. That I'm capable of understanding the phenomena of things but always a little bit too late.

INTERVIEWER: And if you had only one wish?

FRISCH: That those liars who are holding power over others die of a soft, normal, natural disease.

INTERVIEWER: What have you found most satisfying about your achievements?

FRISCH: Not only the so-called success, but that this success created a partnership, a communication with a lot of people whom I don't know personally, people of different generations and nationalities—that's a great satisfaction. I'm astonished about it and very grateful.

INTERVIEWER: What have you been least satisfied with?

FRISCH: I would say . . . you know, it changes all the time. Sometimes, for instance, what bothers me most is that I never had a real overview of my abilities, my capacities. I'm always a little bit blind.

INTERVIEWER: If you could have only one photograph to pass on, with whom would you be pictured, and what would you be doing?

FRISCH: First, I know it wouldn't be a photograph of the young man, but a photo of the old man. Smoking a pipe, or not smoking a pipe, and not in action. Not posing, if possible.

After sex, after coffee, after everything there is to be said—

The hovering and beautiful alphabet as we form our first words after making love.

[17]

And somehow I'm still alive.

Danilo swearing that in the next book he'll do something easier, less ambitious, more suitable to his talent.

So many of the old places: Sabor, Felidia, Trattoria da Alfredo.

Café Un, Deux, Trois.

In Venice. In August. At the mouth of the Saluti. . . . A celebration because *the plague is over!* So much joy.

They were going to go to the river. She brought chayote and plátano.

There was a man whose name was Whistle.

The small light a candle can give. The face flushed.

That's an almond tree. Cherry. Small fig.

A homeless man has fallen asleep in Ann's car on Fourteenth Street when she goes to move it in the morning.

Mr. Tunny and his fourteen-year-old grandson were leaving church when they heard the shots being fired. "He was moving very slowly, very gently." A bullet had entered the boy's cheek and exited the left side of the back of his brain.

I see my light dying.

Our destination in those days was always the sea.

Francesco with his silly film quizzes. Asking me one more time where the word *paparazzi* came from.

The choice is made a little mysteriously, in a superstitious manner, not rationally. Still it is made: ultraviolet light, or radiation,

Chinese herbs.

Danilo puts in a good word for modern American medicine.

INTERVIEWER: If you could remember, could keep forever, just one story, what would it be?

FRISCH: Which one? It would not be the story of my life, or a story I have heard, but a myth. I think it would be the myth of Icarus.

Aldo kept drawing ladders.

Ladders going nowhere, maybe.

It's OK.

My aunt then, wandering, confused, during the war.

We took the overnight train.

We danced to Prince all night long in the circular room. It was 1988. It was France.

You were on holiday.

One night.

It was everything while it lasted.

One night once.

A shining thing.

My father offering pennies for each Japanese beetle.

She sends an envelope of poems.

There is not a day that I do not think of you.

The glittering green of beetles. . . . Hanging on the lip of a yellow rose.

The lemon trees are planted along the garden walls. By and by they will be covered with rush mats, but the orange trees are left in the open. Hundreds and hundreds of the loveliest fruits hang on these trees. They are never trimmed or planted in a bucket as in our country, but stand free and easy in the earth, in a row with their brothers.

Music moves in me. Shapes I've needed to complete. Listen. Listen hard:

I hear a heart beating.

Can it be that our visit was only eight months ago?

I know I am lucky that music moves in me in such a way—and if it has rearranged a few chaotic cells or changed the composition of my blood—but even if it hasn't—still—I have been of course, extraordinarily lucky.

That night the baby was conceived. In a room called Joie de Vivre.

Where you spoke, Anatole, only once, and in a whisper, of freedom and how much you needed the sky and good-bye—

Swinging on the swing. What shall we name her?

Can it be that our visit was only eight months ago? It is so hard to imagine . . . I think even with all the insanity and pain of those days I was happier. I miss you.

xxx B

Sing to me of Paris and of lost things.

I knew a boy named Bernard Reznikoff. Quiet, carrying a stack of books. Blushing. New York City.

Just once I'd like to save Virginia Woolf from drowning. Hart Crane. Primo Levi from falling. Paul Celan, Bruno Schulz, Robert Desnos, and for my parents: Grandma and Grandpa, Uncle Isaac, Uncle Solly, Aunt Sophie, just once.

In the city of New York. Where I taught school, sang songs, watched

[20]

my friends come and go. Climbed the pointy buildings. Marveled at all the lights.

Aldo, building cathedrals with his voice.

A man in a bowler hat disappears into thin air. Grandfather.

She was dressed in a gown of gold satin. Suppose it had been me?

She shudders at the sight of a garter belt as if it were a contraption of supreme torture.

I think of him often: Samuel Beckett learning to fly.

Look for this in my shoe.

He waits for disguised contacts who sometimes never come.

A a. B b.

All the bodies piling up on stage.

C.

Like your father you grew old roses.

Snow falls like music in the late autumn.

Home, before it was divided.

A pretty rough show, then, for someone who came to see nudes, portraits and still lifes. It is made rougher still by the inescapable dates on the labels of the stronger images, all of which come from that hopeful ignorant time when it seemed that all that was involved was a kind of liberation of attitude concerning practices between consenting adults in a society of sexual pluralism. Of course the show has its tenderer moments. There are prints of overwhelming tenderness of Mapplethorpe's great friend Patti Smith. There is a lovely picture of Brice Marden's little girl. It is possible to be moved by a self-portrait of 1980 in which Mapplethorpe shows himself in women's makeup, eager and girlish and almost pubescent in the frail flatness of his/her naked upper body. . . .

Let me describe what my life once was here.

Home before it was divided.

. . . The self-portrait as a young girl remains in my mind as the emblem of the exhibition, and the dark reality that has settled upon the world to which it belongs. One cannot help but think back to Marcel Duchamp's self-representation in *maquillage*, wearing the sort of wide-brimmed hat Virginia Woolf might have worn with a hatband designed by Vanessa, with ringed finger and a fur boa. . . .

Come sit in the morning garden for awhile. Open the map.

With AIDS a form of life went dead, a way of thought, a form of imagination and hope. Any death is tragic and the death of children especially so. . . . But this other death carries away a whole possible world.

A remote chorus of boys.

Shall we take the upper or the lower corniche?

The way the people you loved spoke—expressed themselves in letters, or at the beach, or at the moment of desire.

Maybe I should go now.

No. Please stay.

The smell of rosemary carried in on the fur of Salome.

Reading Italian magazines.

Never forget these things.

As Lorca's biographer said it of him, I say it of you Francesco: You were a "staggering one-man show."

There is not a day I do not think of you.

Mysterious, nocturnal, lunar. And while he loved the morning, the smells, the light, he rarely saw it unless a film demanded he rise at five.

Music assumes a shape in me.

Aida and Mimi lie in a square of morning light.

What a strange and brave world.

We were working on an erotic song cycle.

Danilo and I drinking Stolichnaya until we passed out.

What a beautiful world this is.

Nymphets by the pool.

A favorite Chinese restaurant. The way you held my hand. Steam and ginger. Good news. On the street, rain, and a yellow taxi cab. I love you.

You brush the curls from your face.

Francesco, I remember the trays of colognes, the silk ties, the dark wood, the anisette and grappa. I remember our living room—that elaborate stage set. Me singing Puccini for you and how you wept. Your love of Charlie Chaplin, your tenderness, your exuberance. Madcap in the afternoon.

Francesco, I am dying, maybe.

The nurses at their station: Let me know if you are going to Central Park.

A day of ravioli and Rossellini. And later a little risotto with porcini perhaps.

And I remember, don't you, the burnished lower strings accompanying Butterfly's

[23]

Belated grasping of the situation in the finale.

He tried hard in those days to pepper his conversation with English. To make me laugh.

Put your feet in the straps. Slowly begin to rock forward. . . . Your arms above your head now, he whispers.

When Ana Julia died Carlos was already making the picnic lunch.

You thought you were going to the river, but really you were going somewhere quite else, all along.

My urgency, for you in that apartment vestibule. It should have been obvious, even then

And what in the world were we waiting for? Or trying to stave off, finally?

Everything changed in a moment.

Presto!

An apartment vestibule: "Try not to touch the intercom."

Things are taken away. Think of Ana Julia, flying down the street.

And all the air a solemn stillness holds. Till 8:30 when the cadaverous twanging in the sky begins; the planes going to London. Well, it's an hour still to that. Cows feeding. The elm tree sprinkling its little leaves against the sky. Our pear tree swagged with pears; and the weathercock above the triangular church tower above it. Why try again to make the familiar catalogue from which something escapes. Should I think of death? Last night a great heavy plunge of bomb under the window. So near we both started. A plane had passed dropping this fruit. We went on to the terrace. Trinkets of stars sprinkled and glittering. All quiet. The bombs dropped on Itford Hill. There are two by the river, marked with white wooden crosses, still unburst. I said to L: I don't want to die yet.

Dear Virginia Woolf.

Blue shoes.

Amagansett, Long Island.

Breathe.

Crete.

The daydreaming city of Chloe.

Provincetown, Massachusetts.

Paris, Venice, Roma. Barcelona. Tourrettes-sur-Loup.

Sing to me of lost things.

London, Berlin.

Oh I try to imagine how one's killed by a bomb. I've got it fairly vivid—the sensation: but can't see anything but suffocating nonentity following after. I shall think—oh I wanted another 10 years—not this—

Don't forget to breathe.

Franz, a lover of one night.

He's called the Zodiac Killer because before he shoots he asks your sign. He's looking for birthday boys and girls.

Across the street at Benny Burritos, Latino boys bragging.

All over the world,

They were sent to the left and I was sent to the right.

Instead of France, then Germany, my preferred destinations, I am on a train to the Upper East Side.

Turn right at the dead goat, walk over the bridge of flowers and you are there. That was Crete. Some time ago.

We used to follow the rabbit path. . . .

City officials assure us that they have caught the real Dart Man. And that these others are imitation dart men. Hard to know which is stranger, the passion for hitting women in the buttocks with darts or the passion for imitation.

Marie-Claude, fallen. "I am still very much a one-armed girl. But I am saving just enough strength to hug you when you arrive."

Are the officials trying to convince us now that the imitation darts do not sting as much as the genuine article?

Please, please take best care my friends. I cannot bear the thought that either of you should be hurt, ever.

Meanwhile the Zodiac Killer is looking for a Leo.

You've really got to wonder sometimes.

The city you describe does not exist, says Kublai Khan.

But, yes, it does.

My heart

The return to a city after many years away.

Dear Ava,

I wow'ed 'em, or so they actually said. No offer yet, but February 15. And then they wow'ed me too, a bit: the tropics are (especially after Chicago's stark midwinter) heady stuff. And the kids were nice (and then I'd have graduate students) and the faculty ditto. It's a den of Proust scholars. That seems all right. And I sat this morning in South Beach and thought of you: it's full of Eurotrash and models and I saw some of the most magnificent creatures I've seen in my life!

We call her the false niece because he is sleeping with her, and it would not do if she were his real niece. And so today, bumping into him up by Sloan Kettering, How is the false niece, Jonathan? I ask.

In the photograph, his hand on my shoulder.

It was when you still had a hand.

Let's travel.

What I would like: for you to have grown old and back into the role of the youthful Rudolfo, with all your wisdom and wit and innocence.

Your intelligence.

To hear you call me ma bohème. Just once more.

Sing to me, dear friend. My heart,

A rare bird.

Carlos, who adored her, and asked her to hold on a little longer. He would sit by the river with her. They would rent a boat.

But one can only hold on for so long.

I'm taking charge of this situation, I say out loud to Madame Butterfly, the cat.

At the bar I try to tell a shapely story. I notice people are listening. Trying to glean this or that from my odd monologue.

Someone's eyes cloud over as I say the part about the apartment vestibule, remembering:

Tell me what time of day was it—and what was the weather like?

Across the room at a party. . . .

My heart is breaking.

I swam across the lake. He followed me in a boat.

Scotch in a tall glass.

Breathe.

Virtual Reality sets in. A headset.... Some business about a headset.

I looked left and they were gone.

You want to wear a shield over your heart, when you finally understand how fragile it is.

A helmet.

Start with how his hair caught the light.

You want to wear a shield. But not really.

August and the beach. The sun is becoming something that will burn us alive. We're not far from the human torch stage.

How can we live without you?

Charlie, just in from Paris, discussing *Sex, Lies and Videotape.*

I'm taking control of this situation, I say, getting up and putting a few Diet Iams in Aida's dish.

Reports from a country called By a Thread.

A country called What Happened to the Ozone?

He wrote in code

How can we live without

I still love you, Broken Sky.

Germany

A Sherry Lehman truck stops in front of the window. Could it be a delivery for me? I once loved somebody who loved Sherry Lehman. We'd go after the museum. 679 Madison Avenue.

Prewar Paris, irretrievably lost.

He sits down to write.

Name changed. Address changed.

Danilo explains his books are questions of survival of personality. They are not written to get or keep an audience. The maker has made them to please himself.

I might look up and—

To live in New York is something like living in the whole world simultaneously.

What this time, Ann, was just a benign cyst, at any point could become something else. We know that. We are holding on, and yes, by a thread.

The elm tree sprinkling its little leaves against the sky.

I remember Anatole just before he put on his flying suit and waved good-bye.

I'm taking charge of this situation, she said.

Wittig's message here is that action—the act of writing, of creating new language—is the overflow not only of words, but of the reality and the traditions these words have fashioned and perpetuated.

His cloak of clouds. Anatole Forget.

1 November

Dear Ava,

Today is, of course, a holiday in Europe. People go to the cemetery and cover graves with evergreen branches and place bouquets of chrysanthemums. Outside the streets are almost

[29]

deserted. I went for a walk in the park near where I live a little while ago and I crossed a lot of fathers out pushing baby carriages.

As the envelope has already indicated, I am writing to you from Krakow in Poland where I have come to live.

How very much I miss you now.

But what kind of charge was I taking?

In the Café Pourquoi Pas, in the Café Tout Va Bien, in the Café Le Club, where we seemed to live then. We were living a sort of café life.

In Paris seventy years ago—

Don't think I've forgotten Marcel Proust, that we walked down the boulevard together in what I can only describe as a moment of perfect happiness.

En plein air.

Francesco sends turbans of the most astounding colors in the overnight mail.

Ana Julia, eighty-five, on one of her false deathbeds: Don't think because this life was brief, that it wasn't absolutely everything.

She finds herself on a foreign coast.

I loved your grandson Carlos. His wild ways and hair. Until the wildness in one of us, or maybe both of us got played out. Went one step further than where we could reasonably live.

And we were all for living, then.

My third and last husband, Carlos.

Tequila under the pomegranate tree.

Stampeding of horses and feet.

There are certain passages, written toward the end of Proust's life and inserted into his text, in particular a whole section of the *Temps retrouvé*, in which hurried by a sense of impending death—

Let me know if you are going.

One night once.

Could he, I wonder now, have ever been mine?

A quiet but complete nervous breakdown—

Zoo heen kan gaan.

The longing for stories. What is closure? What cultural and gender-related assumptions do we bring to any given set of—

Assignment: Rewrite *Death in Venice* as a feminist text.

For a short time no one was sure whether or not the war had ended.

Samuel Beckett waiting for reinforcements. It's the war. But no reinforcements come.

One hundred love letters, written by hand.

He was going to make Dante's *Inferno* into a film. You're not, I said. I was twenty then. Studying for my master's in comparative lit.

The maid had stolen the blue satin wedding shoes while Ana Julia slept. Woken from a dream where the exact same thing was happening, Ana Julia rose and flew down the street after her.

And the next day in Ana Julia's house—twenty-five viejas saying the rosary.

For where she was going, she needed those shoes.

Along the boulevard,

I am losing the vague dread.

[31]

On the strategic island of Crete, on fertile soil, on ancient, holy, bitter, proud—

If we are lucky, when we are young, we learn that we must die. In this department I was lucky.

Treblinka—a rather musical word.

If my calculations are anywhere near accurate it is perfectly possible that while Ana Julia was retrieving her shoes, I was being handed the written results of my blood tests. I believe I closed my eyes and—

Confetti falls on my face the way it did that Bastille Day.

The results, written in blood.

The mother accepts her beautiful homosexual son. On her face, worry, love. He seems very young, she said of Aldo's last lover. Trembling. Nineteen.

He sang like a songbird. Always, always, she said.

Rain and *L'Avventura* and your Mad Max impersonations.

We were working on an erotic song cycle.

I got to sing. I got to kiss you on the cheek.

Ava Klein, your chances are slim.

I imagine Ana Julia rose from her sleepy hammock and flew down the dusty road like some great bird.

And Carlos says, through the static,

Twenty-five viejas saying the rosary.

I held your trembling hand.

We played the games of folded paper, of Questions and Answers, of Jack of Hearts, of Pony and Innuendo.

I don't know how we could have hesitated.

They carried her through the streets. The white bleached cemetery, all angels and crosses.

It is given.

Along the boulevard: Limoges. Lalique. Blown glass from Biot.

It is taken back.

Almond. Cherry. Small fig.

Ash.

Brilliant sunlight. Rain without warning. Then snow, in the Joie de Vivre room.

Snow piling high outside Rizzoli's where we held Italian magazines and wept.

I can't believe your wingspan!

When you begin the book: "Steel-blue and light, ruffled by a soft, scarcely perceptible crosswind, the waves of the Adriatic streamed against the imperial squadron . . ." but by the time you close it, having just read the final sentence, Ana Julia has died. One thousand and one things change the meaning of any book on any given reading.

At the next table, talk of Greece.

Still cheap . . . Feta cheese.

I could not as it turns out get on a plane to France, or Germany, or any plane, that day. Rare blood disease, demanding as the doctor said, *immediate action.*

New York.

Yes, but what are my chances?

[33]

Danilo brings me an aquarium. Tells me stories. Aquarium was the code word for—

Undeniably, the chemotherapy makes me most resemble them then.

What about wigs? So as not to be ghoulish. Rachel and Phillip. Sophie. Sol. So many bad memories.

The code word for the KGB.

We could sing.

She rose from her hammock. Running down the long dirt road fast, then faster, to catch that scoundrel, ungrateful girl, after all she'd done.

Good morning, Ava Klein.

You are a rare bird.

The man in the café moves his hand and three purple blotches are revealed. The once rare Kaposi's sarcoma. The once nearly unheard of, never seen.

The sun, now something that can burn us alive.

The woman in the wig shop suggests a dark brown, for a change.

I close my eyes and see her leaning over a stove to light a cigarette. It was a Fassbinder movie. He was still alive then.

How does this strike you as a beginning?

In my 340, the Russian Novel, we considered Anna's dilemma.

"Gorbachev . . . Latvia . . ." Danilo says dreamily over the hospital phone. "Ha—" what is it? "Ha— Havel."

Try not to be so upset.

Aunt Sophie, my mother's only sister, black hair and such red lips.

Must she survive everyone?

Ana Julia: Qué linda! on our wedding day.

Maria Regina: Bellissima! on our wedding day.

Marie-Claude and Emma: Ava, you are a picture! on my wedding day.

He called me Beatrice. A forehead so white. The color of pearl.

Learning to fly.

Nothing to regret now. Not even the child we kept putting off, Carlos.

I sent you an olive branch in the mail. So that there might be peace.

Beckett waiting for disguised contacts who sometimes did not come.

Women in turbans.

Ana Julia praying to the Virgin for children.

What is wrong with you, Ava Klein?

The effects of chemotherapy in the childbearing years.

My uncle wore a pink triangle through the gray of

Treblinka—a rather musical word.

How have I ended up back here, again?

The only industrialized country in the world, besides South Africa, without health care.

Vienna la sera.

I call all the cats in: Madame Butterfly, Aida, Lulu, Parsifal, Salome.

I met Franz during a production of *Salome*. "Wer ist dies Weib, das mich ansieht?"

One night once.

Who is this girl who is so curious? you whispered.

It is me, Franz, Ava Klein, in a wig.

She puts her lips on the cup. He puts his lips on the cup. She bites the ripe and delicious fruit. He puts his mouth to the same place and sucks the juice. "Wer ist dies Weib, das mich ansieht?"

He casts one veil, then another from her.

Thirty A.D.

One night once.

I was your Cunning Little Vixen. You were my Forester, longing for animals. One look was enough. It took one touch.

I would have married you, after just one night. Had I not already been married at the time. I was still very much in love, you probably recall. Madame Forget, you'd called me, and entered again that long rivalry between the German and the French. As surely Anatole would have, had he been there: both sides, condescending, adversarial, dismissive.

Madame Forget—or perhaps I should consider it: how's this? Try this: Frau Müller, then?

I remember those endless, seamless days with you, Anatole, at the café by the sea.

As much as I loved him, it was your mother and her lover, Emma, whom I could not give up, never give up.

I am afraid I am very much a one-armed girl.

All the personal pronouns—j/e, m/on, m/a, m/es—are split to emphasize the disintegration of the self that occurs every time women speak male language.

Are there any questions?

Monique Wittig.

The Empire State Building talks to the people of its city in colors, in colored lights. Green for the Irish, yellow for the hostages, and for the first time—lavender for gay men and lesbians.

It's red, white and blue the day after the fire fighters save it from burning down. A bad fire on its fifty-first floor. A thank you in lights. Its hurt side exposed.

Beloved son. Devoted brother. Cherished friend.

Aldo.

The paper says that the smog and haze have made it impossible anymore to see. Once we could see for ninety miles in any direction. And if all man-made substances could be wrung from the atmosphere, once again we'd be able to see for ninety miles.

A terrible longing, a nostalgia, a restlessness. For air. For ocean. For the ability to see.

Imagine what Ana Julia might have seen then.

Set me free.

I will never forget when the traveling circus came to town. Little Carlos had never seen such a thing.

Ninety miles behind us. Ninety miles ahead of us. Ninety miles in any direction. I focus my mind's eye:

Genoa, Italy, 1970.

You have Italy in your soul, Ava Klein, Francesco said on the night he proposed. He bounded up the sea-soaked steps.

Chianti.

I find myself indoors more, gnawing, like Francesco's grandfather

Spaghetti Puttanesca: And afterwards, grappa and another anisette biscuit.

Danilo plans a short trip to Eastern Europe with the news to his friends: You are going to fail.

I glimpse the woman in the wig in a store window and laugh.

And as I continue down the boulevard now: marzipan, Fabergé eggs, beads of every shape, Limoges, lace.

A man in the house he plays with serpents he writes
he writes when the night falls to Germany your golden hair

Franz in his thick accent whispers, Ava Klein, you are a rare bird, and he puts his hand under my dress.

We drink and we drink you.

I was on my way to Germany

Without music, as the piece has been choreographed—

Open your mouth, Ava Klein.

Dancing with him in the heat. Hallucinatory, tattooed.

Now, to walk even a few blocks you need Sunblock #30.

Brazil. A feather headdress. A farewell to the flesh.

Venice.

The way her voice rises to say, Such gorgeous sun! And the way the light hit both of them at a certain hour in the garden seat that swung back and forth and back and forth. The smell of herbs. And he slowly moving his hand up my leg, through lace when the women retired from the heat. A lizard. A cat. An orange poppy.

It was a kind of paradise.

Emma says herbs—like the man's name—in her British accent. Hundreds of Herbs.

I am going to fall on the floor like Ana Julia, Tia Dora, ninety-three, says. Mama, it's not only you, Blanquita says. We're all going to fall on the floor.

They were going to rent a car. They were going to go to the river.

The man named Whistle now leading the procession, and Milagro, a Down's syndrome child, for fifty years.

Ana Julia, ninety-five, and flying.

In the end, all the people of the town chasing the maid down the street for those shoes.

The story having spread quickly through the small village.

He would wrench himself out of a sound sleep to ask if I was faithful, at the exact moment I was touching myself and thinking of someone else. As I have been known to do.

You can't believe the fruit here! Come soon if you can.

In the village all the talk is of Ana Julia's daughter, swindling the money kept under her mattress for years so that she might have a new nose. And maybe get some pouches off.

I like to think of Ana Julia flying down the dirt road and cursing.

How did we live then, do you remember?

I wonder if her daughter, Carlos' mother, will get the face she's after, after all.

A sort of wayward Hispanic Jackie Kennedy.

Something called the Swami Team has been brought in to deal with the Zodiac.

Yes, but who is looking for George Bush: "serial killer," as the posters say? "One AIDS death every twelve minutes."

Keith Haring's radiant baby crawling through the dark city.

Words are less integers than points in a continuum. Indeed one might well describe the structure of the lyric as the expression of the interval.

Danilo, I say, cheer up. You don't have to break literary ground every time you step on it.

It happened, bus-pas, Tía Dora says and snaps her fingers. Like that.

The lepidopterist tiptoes toward the unknown species.

I remember Pierrot le Fou, in the moment he "stopped painting definite things."

And satin shoes,

The white geometry of the Piscine Municipale, just to name a few.

The mind cuts loose.

The mind was a kind of paradise.

The body gets up and dances.

All along I have just wanted to be free.

In the Musée Picasso in the town of Antibes, in the room called Joie de Vivre.

And I have come to relinquish that most modern of stances: uncertainty. I am certain now of what will happen.

In between treatments, a new project: to help Ann with her dating service questionnaire.

First I suggest she change her name: Anais.

First question.
Q. What are your hobbies, Anais?
How about—A: Designing eggs in the manner of the Fabergés of Russia.

Q: What are your hobbies?
A: Matchbox collections. (Destroyed in a fire.)

Q: What is your favorite animal, Anais?
A: A dog.

No, let us say a gazelle.

Q: What are your goals?
A: To see the entire world.

Q: What do you want?
A: To live a few more years.

Q: What do you fear?
A: Wigs.

Q: What do you fear?
A: The desert.

Q: What do you fear most?
A: A simple game of Hide and Seek.

And somewhere I realize that I must stay alive for you.

I don't know what would make one person do that to another.

Fill in the blanks:
I dislike most _____.

I am happiest when _____.

To sing the endless variations on the themes we set up.

Q: What is your secret fantasy?
A: To be the first woman to make a solo flight over the Red Sea in a glider.

How's that, Anais?

Because everyone, after all, wants to find their perfect match.

As I was answering the last question about the secret fantasy, as I was choosing exactly where I wished to fly over, the nurse came in to take more blood. Maybe I did not really mean to say the Red Sea.

Red Village. Red Dog. Make a wish.

I think of the infinite beginnings, middles and ends to a life.

Where Francesco and I sat on the porch of the Last Chance Saloon, deep in the American summer, and wept.

If you could make one wish

Q: Tell me what did you think was beautiful there?

The intricate pattern on the scarf on the head of a Yugoslavian woman is beautiful, and the way you tried to hide your disappointment at not winning the prize so as not to spoil the evening is beautiful. And the small bird as it arrives elegantly on the plate. And how surely if I have loved anyone it is you. And how you even understood in the end, why we could not make it work, despite love—despite everything we had going.

And so perhaps the inverse too is true. While it absolutely seems certain that the party is over—who can know such a thing for sure?

I am only a little tired, like everyone.

Presto.

One never feels very far from the sea.

I am looking at the work done during the artist's early late period. It
is called *The Yugoslavian Scarf*. It is called *The Passage of the Red Sea*.

He bounded up the sea-soaked steps.

Fill in the blanks.

And I realize I must stay alive for you.

Ecco.

It was Rome. I was twenty. You were making a film of the *Inferno*. I
laughed imagining the task. I was a graduate student. I held your
giant Roman hand. You pressed me against a broken wall,

It was paradise.

It was what we were.

Close up you look like a statue.

Ether floats in the air.

They drank the gas like milk.

What did you think was beautiful there?

For she was, or became increasingly, a woman with nothing to lose.

Uncle Solly lifts a dark cup

No—

In a dress, to his lips.

Bratislava.

I think it must be very beautiful there.

[43]

I went to write a longish line of the erotic song cycle with Jean-Luc, if that was his name.

Do you remember this part? We were standing in the snow outside Rizzoli's when you told me.

We were walking into the fire called July.

Tyger! Tyger! burning bright.

A little bit longer,

Soon it will be dark.

He describes a quiet but complete nervous breakdown at the MacDowell Colony,

If you only had one wish

Blow out the candles.

Courage

Yes, I am positive, he said, that day in the snow. Holding Italian magazines in the street.

For some time no one was sure whether or not the war had ended.

A pot au feu, in cold weather. By the fire.

Breathe.

Close up you are exactly like a statue.

The child draws the letter A.

Carnaval. . . .

And dancing, dancing.

The light in your eyes.

Venice. Rio. Quebec.

I miss the old days, when we were all there together.

The voice of a woman and a cello. . . .

And the one-armed man comes up to the flower shop and the days go by endlessly, endlessly, pulling you into the future. And the florist says: white lily.

Our original happiness.

Ava Klein, Anatole smiles, petting my feather headdress. You are a rare bird. La Belle Province. 1980. Carnaval.

An extremely rare blood cancer.

Is Danilo then my final lover? Have I saved with some purpose his sad and hopeful country for last?

Come in.

This is a part written for my doctor, who is doing what he can.

You are an *extremely rare* bird, Ava Klein.

Sometimes I think, Dr. Oppenheim, I might have married you.

Imagine a flock of brave little children—and those two small coffins at the end—made entirely of light.

The blind poet passes in his hot air balloon,

He sees: From Brooklyn to Manhattan from Manhattan to Brooklyn, from the Lower East Side to the Upper East Side, from the West Village to Sloan Kettering, in the taxi, on the radio, Willie Colón, José Luis Rodríguez, Miguel singing, and singing, and driving and singing,

And Sloan Kettering along.

Ramon Fernandez, tell me, if you know.

I know a place we can still go.

We used to take the rabbit path.

A stray cat named Della. The next-door neighbors in that seaside town in winter, keeping track of her. Signs on the doors. Della In. Della Out. Della left by a summer resident.

By my calculations Ana Julia was just being born as Samuel Beckett was learning to fly.

And in Germany: How we loved to go to the park. Father would do his funny walk that made all of us laugh so hard we fell in the grass.

The first tests—the first clue of anything really wrong—being read, the blood already separating into its wrong parts as Ana Julia was slipping on her recaptured shoes.

The child learns her alphabet.

I know a place we can still go.

We were working on an erotic song cycle. It was called *A Place We Can Still Go.*

And six hours ahead of us my dear friends, Marie-Claude and Emma, were preparing the little cottage by the gray cliffs for me.

This is for you, because there was no other way at the time to get to you.

And again it will be winter, and Rodolfo will take Mimi's hand in the garret in the Latin Quarter in Paris of the 1830s on the stage of the Metropolitan Opera.

O soave fanciulla.

Parsifal purring on my lap.

A highly experimental drug for a very rare disease arrives from Tunisia.

Pears poached in red wine.

French mirabelle plums and white peaches.

Olives hang like earrings in late August.

Strawberries in December. Black tulips. Basil in winter.

Something so—

Something rare.

Douceurs de la vie. . . .

I want to live.

I am aiming for France but I touch Tunisia instead.

Medina. Souks. Strange new words.

Keep the light on. Don't turn out the light. I love your mouth. I want to see you when you come.

Matisse, mid-career, in Morocco. Paul Klee, André Gide in Tunis. Everything white. White light. White domes. Bouka—a white alcohol distilled from figs.

And la plage.

A white clay oven. A million swallows at sunset. Let's get lost in the patterns of rugs. A minaret. A citadel. Swirling dancers. The gate leading to the mosque. Open me.

Let's travel. Let's go now.

Beads on the neck of a beautiful, dark woman and across the bay little beads of light. And pills like pearls I take at morning and at night.

The pull and drag of the tide.

Orange tiger lilies against a white house in summer.

Je t'embrasse tendrement.

I have not forgotten the lilies or the pressed violets.

I looked left and they were gone.

Sophie, Sol, Mother, Father.

She had a voice like a songbird.

Marie-Claude shows me how to make a pot a feu. For fall.

Try to understand, you say in French, from high up.

We loved the Cours Mirabeau in Aix-en-Provence, lined by double plane trees.

"The tanks had not yet come." That was how you began the story, Danilo.

Without realizing it, Kundera says, the individual composes his life according to the laws of beauty even in times of greatest distress.

Snow covers the beach.

This I think is true, despite Danilo's dismissal of Kundera and his theories of history.

He fills the aquarium with small black fish.

The first thing I see when I open my eyes. And don't they look exactly like

Music?

We were working on an erotic song cycle. It was called *Come Sit by
the Aquarium for Awhile*

And sing.

Nine A.M.: time for a treatment, Ava Klein.

Yvette Poisson in a fuzzy pale sweater, returned now, at this desolate
moment, as the nurse wheels me up the cold hall—and the ease at
which I arrive at this: Yvette Poisson dancing.

You were wearing a dress without straps. You were quite burned by
the sun.

Tell me again the story of your love affair with Philip. Start with the
way his hair caught the light.

I can try to complete it in my head.

That perfect purring comfort. To do when I get out: feline leukemia
shots for everyone.

Bend your arm, Ava Klein, for the nurse.

We were working on an erotic song cycle. It was called *Pavane for a
Dead Princess*.

Madame Butterfly, Norma, Aida, Parsifal, Mimi, viens. Viens ici!

In my diamonded hospital sheath and tiara. In my royal bed.

But what rule of beauty is there here at work?

Don du sang.

Now that you've reminded me of that single night long ago—

Here is my arm. I want to live.

His name was Jean-Luc. He had barged in on the small dinner party we were having en plein air. He was already quite drunk.

How is this for a beginning?

Anatole was dead then—nearly an entire season, already.

He said he had been watching you for a long time. We laughed.

How terribly he wanted to be understood, to be taken seriously. He was discussing, he was trying to discuss Marxism and language or something like that with us. We were drinking our gins, or whatever it was we drank then. You were quite burned by the sun.

I was burned from too much sun. I remember, Aldo, the bottles of pastes and lotions you lined up for me in the kitchen. Aloe, other things, a sort of white goo, a tonic.

We were feeling desperate and middle-aged. Even though we were still young, quite young. I had almost forgotten that night completely until just now, Aldo—

You looked at him as if you were seeing right through him. Through to his essential, his strangest self, which he tried alternately to reveal and to hide.

Later in the circular room, we danced for hours to Prince. He pulled me toward him. He pushed me away. I have a woman and a child, he whispered over and over, in broken English.

It must have been what he wanted. He must have wanted to touch a boundary, to feel some limit.

He watched me dance away.

You were wearing a white dress without straps. You must have smelled like lavender when you finally got up from the field with him in the early hours of morning.

I never told you, Aldo whispers, but I was in love with that stranger too.

Aldo, to hear your voice again so vividly in my head!

And you sent me to him, Aldo, in lotions and creams.

In the unlikely event. . . .

A Calisson d'Aix on my tongue.

Half a shell from a coco tree Ana Julia used to wash herself with.
That shell held water. At rest now. A coco shell—inside it a comb.
The comb that held her hair. The relics of a life.

Let us not forget, ever forget such things.

The fish now, in the configuration of the C Major Quintet.

So much precision and tenderness and intimacy in one piece.

But you are married, I thought, I said to the stranger. You have a
woman and child.

Keep the light on.

Take me from behind this time.

Language for women is closely linked with sexuality for Cixous. She
believes that because women are endowed with a more passive and
consequently more receptive sexuality, not centered on the penis,
they are more open than men to create liberated forms of discourse.

Overheard, bits of remembered things,

In letters, or on the beach

How I can be walking that path again if I concentrate. Holding your
hand. The perfect leaves of the French oak. Rue de Marché. Rue de
Beaujolais.

Take me from behind this time.

Or at the moment of desire.

[51]

In the photo we had on our dresser then—Ana Julia, thirty, beautiful, in full native regalia.

The ideal, or the dream, Cixous writes, would be to arrive at a language that heals as much as it separates.

This is for you, Marie-Claude and Emma, because there was no other way at the time, to get to you. This is for you, my dear troubled Anatole.

I have not forgotten.

The painter on the side of the road painting trees from a dream forest.

You can't believe how beautiful it is here. . . . All day we work, take walks, eat or drink. Sing. I have made friends with a few of the Moroccans.

We were working on an erotic song cycle. It was called *Toward a Female Subject.*

Oh, c'est bien, ça!

I miss you. The stone wall, the way the swing swung.

Cap d'Antibes.

What is simple and ordinary comes back. A kiss behind the ear. A kiss on a back street.

Silly things. Glowworm and her son Dreamboat in a peapod. This is how we passed the days. Just children.

Jeux d'enfants.

Twenty-three, twenty-four, twenty-five, twenty-six. . . .

And in winter the memory of heat. And in summer, the cold, the obliterating white. In the rain—bright light.

Dear Ava,

I just received your letter yesterday, and I decided to respond immediately since your name was moving to the top of my list of people I must soon write to. I too have often thought of you during the long dark months of the Polish winter. (Is there a country more gray on earth than Poland?) Today it is snowing. This is unusual because most of the month of March has been quite mild, and it was weeks ago that I put away my fox hat (yes, I have a fox hat—a "toque" as the French say—it is a beautiful hat that I bought when I first arrived in Krakow in the days when prices were more reasonable. In France or the U.S. it would have cost me about ten times more).

I miss you.

The ideal or the dream would be to arrive at a language that heals as much as it separates.

It was Christmas Eve Day. I wore bells.

How does this strike you as a beginning?

I remember how my parents would weep uncontrollably and without warning, on a summer day, or in the car on the way to school, or during a simple game of Hide and Seek. But not that day. I called them at the summerhouse. Rare blood disease. No known cure. Maybe only weeks.

We thought more and more cats might be the solution to our unhappiness. We dreamed them, named them. "Norma," I called in my sleep,

Where are those voluptuous, sorrowful songs? The lit temple? the jewels? The things I would have liked to have known. No—the things I needed to know.

Come quickly, my mother says, there are finches at the feeder.

Not yet, Dr. Oppenheim. On the slight possibility that I should survive.

Only if we assume that a poet constantly strives to liberate himself from borrowed styles in search of reality is he dangerous, Milosz

[53]

says. In a room where people unanimously maintain a conspiracy of silence, one word of truth sounds like a pistol shot.

It is the bullet meant for you.

The jury's not in yet.

He carries a white cat.

I think he is a cloud now.

In lieu of flowers

Always one more thing to say.

I suppose I am lucky not to be able to feel the daily betrayals of my body that Dr. Oppenheim assures me are taking place. This perfect traitor that has afforded me so much pleasure, which has served me well. I remember. . . .

In the unlikely event.

He grew roses.

It is given. It is taken back.

She sang like a bird.

Let me know if you are going—

During these long dark months of the Polish winter, I often asked myself what the hell I was doing in this place. It still all remains very mysterious, but I do think there has been an underlying sense to all of this. As I write, I am sitting in the recently refurbished "Katiwarnia" of the Royal Hotel—a beautiful, turn-of-the-century hotel, set on the edge of old Krakow and new. Across the road is "Wawel." This is where the city of Krakow began, on a hill overlooking the Vistula and its early king was named Krak (thus Krakow). This was also the headquarters of the German occupation government during WWII and the SS often wined and dined in this hotel.

The poet draws the letter L. The poet draws the letter D.

I think of what we held close and why.

The poet writes love. The poet writes death.

Leo, then Virgo, then Libra, then Scorpio. I am a Pisces. Vital information in this case.

I am only thirty-nine. But I am only thirty-nine, Dr. Oppenheim.

As if the Zodiac Killer, or the body, can be reasoned with.

Twenty-six:

You are married, Ava Klein, and you are trying to make this marriage work.

No. Not tonight.

Try and hold off a little bit.

Excellent advice.

I have not forgotten—

Lizards slither. Tell me what you want.

She calls: Your wife and my husband are having an affair.

He ties me to a tree. Repent. He puts me on a short leash.

The cure that time, Carlos, after betrayal, after discovery, was a little garlic soup. And we felt patched up—one more time.

The young, clear-thinking Ana Julia wore a piece of meat under her arm all day, as she toiled, as she slaved, then at night fed it to the one she had chosen so that he would fall hopelessly and faithfully in love with her forever.

An old spell.

Feed me.

An hour and a half delay. The passenger carrying a "mono" on the plane. No animals allowed, only children. And she insisting it is her baby, and throwing it kisses and wrapping it again and again in its swaddling clothes, and its tail, at first contained by the infant garb, slowly, as the debate deepens, unfurls. We were on our way to Spain then. Of course. Where else?

A monkey for a son.

Ana Julia shrugs, because it's perfectly normal.

I make no apologies for these texts, Danilo says. They are un-orthodox, but only slightly and refute I hope all that has been simplistic and inadvertently false, but false nonetheless in my work thus far.

To share a twelve-franc bottle of wine with you again.

Cixous: We've been turned away from our bodies, shamefully taught to ignore them, to strike them with that stupid sexual modesty.

I make no apologies.

Jessie Helms, health insurance, the NEA, no family leave, all perfectly good reasons to get out of here *as soon as possible.*

Do you smoke, Ava Klein?

Do you drink?

Is there a history of serious illness in your family?

Van Gogh's last words: Zoo heen kan gaan.

I can go then.

This is the way to go, or

I want to go home. Depending on the translation you prefer.

Sleeplessness. Bad dreams. A little tree in a dish.

Zoo heen kan gaan. Zoo heen kan gaan.

To Eliot a poem presents itself as a rhythm, not as a set of words.

Sing me a Yiddish song.

There is a necessary melancholy that comes over one when it is realized that there will remain places unseen, books unread, people untouched. Ferocious, hungry, amorous as I imagined myself to be—

In vain, she tried to cross the desert.

Tent of blood. And sand.

I am restless a little. Ready to go there.

Dance the horah, then, just once.

Aldo, do you remember that beautiful remote chorus of boys?

The *War Requiem*, the Wilfred Owen text, and how we thought we would escape all harm?

I think of that grandfather's efficient, pointy teeth. His love for all things that end.

A remote chorus of boys.

To be sung:

I was never much interested in American fascists or Italian fascists, the Austrians, the Nazis or the neo-Nazis, or the skinheads, like so many of my Jewish friends. I was not particularly interested in the Aryan sons of the people who killed people whose names I know.

[57]

I never wanted to embrace that evil or some idea of it. I have never felt bad about surviving. I have never been to Auschwitz, never been to Treblinka. No all along

To be sung: I have just wanted to live.

But it occurs to me, Franz, at this late hour, that you might have been one of them.

We were working on an erotic song cycle. It was called *Flirting in the Life Café*.

Not to be misleading of course. So I see you are into kinky sex, the advertising executive smirked the next morning, having gotten just the slightest intimation the night before. But something about "into kinky sex" bothered me. He had committed a sin of language and I never saw him again.

Cixous: Other strange things happen: each page I write could be the first page of the book. Each page is completely entitled to be the first page. How is this possible?

He was trying to sell low-tar cigarettes to the Third World. Or maybe it was beans to the Americans.

Always one more thing to say.

It occurs to me, Franz—

The slow movements of the later Schubert.

Sing to me, my love.

It's hard to walk.

Have you left the key in its old hiding spot?

But, it is not, after all, that summer anymore.

This is the way to go.

I'm feeling, she said rather matter-of-factly, the tug of the drop.

I'd like you tonight up against the wall.

Danilo reports:
The change occurred over eleven years in a population of guppies in Trinidad. Said Dr. Futuyama: To my knowledge this is the first such experiment to look for a real evolutionary change in life history under natural conditions. It provides a very nice confirmation of basic theory that was based on pure thought and mathematics. The result is really quite lovely.

So give me your hand.

Guppies in Trinidad. Black music.

For the dating service questionnaire, Anais. Why not?

In the terrible, in the terrifying, in the terror—at night—they still had Schubert in their throats.

We had made a plan to work on an erotic song cycle because "you are a poet in your blood, Ava Klein," the young composer said.

Songs the blood sings.

When Francesco found out about our hours of necessary research, he destroyed what he believed were the tapes of our work.

Vienna la sera.

But he had instead destroyed *Turandot* and *Tosca*. And he wept.

Will night never come?

The same corner you now turn in bright light, in heat, and in some fear, you once turned in snow and the mind calls that up, reminded of the way we pressed magazines to our chests.

High winds. Cold.

Olives hang like earrings in late August.

A cat named Eros.

And how the coffee smelled.

This grove of olive trees has been here for thousands of years.

All I have, Danilo says, is this notebook. And you.

Don't be so silly.

In Spain, in a golden square, she sang for joy, as she let him go.

Handed him back his crown of thorns. His leash. His too short leash.

Averted successfully for once his deep, sexual glare.

Food we could not eat.

Her contempt for authority brought her a kind of joy, a kind of raison d'être, a second life.

My mother, alone, standing above what she believes is her sister Sophie's grave.

I picture it quiet there and high up.

Sophie's grave. The luxury to be able to form these words.

They kept her what can only be called plump, for their needs—certainly for their needs, so that she could sing. So that she could

Songbird. Love boat.

My mother was beautiful. She could sing like a bird.

She would not approve of me telling you this.

She was not yet twenty. She was beautiful.

In the unlikely event that I should survive.

Nothing to be ashamed of.

Japanese beetles, a penny apiece.

Shiny hair on the pillow next to me: it was mine and not mine. Detached from my head. Beautiful wavy hair.

Bad dreams.

Come back. All I have, Danilo says, is this notebook, and you.

The shapes I can still make out—my parents—watering and watering the gardens—upstate New York.

Bad dreams.

Saint Thomas on his deathbed: Everything I wrote seems to me straw.

I open the paper and see the ship, the *Scandinavian Star*, on fire in the North Sea.

You were all I ever wanted.

Sarraute demonstrates that the genuine response to art is on an immediate and personal level. It is essentially a wordless conversation between the author and the reader and his or her willingness to assume the same responsibilities and prerogatives as the author.

The whole world on fire.

On the tiny TV: the president draws a line in the sand.

Look for this in my shoe.

To Moses the stutterer, no words are available with which to articulate the essential, the election of suffering that is history, and the real presence of God as it was signified to him in the tautology out of the Burning Bush. The fire there is the only true speech.

The child practices the letter A. Make a mountain peak. And then cross it. A.

And when Uncle Alan was dying, they brought him a DuMont, the first television in the neighborhood, the first television for miles. Everyone over. Uncle Alan hungrily taking in his first and last glimpses. Saying good-bye each night. In the static, in the deep blue flickering light.

Fire light.

The little men in the field throwing a ball. The last thing he sees.

Tell me another story. Huddled around the fire of the alphabet.

Treblinka, he whispers into the flickering—

The bastards. A rather musical word, don't you think?

Look for this—

Everyone's charting the Zodiac. Cryptic clues and a calendar. Operation Watchdog.

Strike two.

A fucking musical word, Uncle Alan says.

Everyone now being asked their sign. All of New York like one big singles bar.

Hey, what's your sign? The passion for imitation great. And a lot easier than coming up with your own original crime.

Every guy now of a certain physical description, suddenly allowed to feel like the Zodiac Killer, famous. 5' 11". Middle-aged. Black.

Carlos says Tía Dora seems to be walking better, faster, having passed now safely that dangerous ninety-one-year mark. Ana Julia, it seems, has scared the death out of her.

Lazlo becomes Fred, Beta becomes Frank, José—Big Joey, and they stand like that on the corner of West Houston and Broadway, Fred, Frank, and Joey, asking each other what signs they are.

Fred, a Cancer, in the most trouble presently.

The man down the hall who is so sick swears he is seeing more and more cats.

Those cats are real, Hazy Dave. Those cats are mine.

And more and more books; that's true too. For both of us. Danilo, a kind of bookmobile.

Because we can still translate black marks on a white paper. There's a code on the page that can take you places.

The writer's morality, Paz says, does not lie in the subjects he deals with or the assignments he sets forth, but in his behavior toward language. . . .

I am losing the vague dread.

He bounded up the sea-soaked steps.

It's quiet here. High up.

Francesco, I am dying maybe.

People listen more attentively to me these days.

Without inventing a single character, without inventing happenings of more significance than his own simple reality, without taking refuge in inventions of any kind—

Your hand that pulled this very shade down, that cupped my breast.

[63]

That now rests in the bed sheet.

A story without a message. He has none to give, and yet he is alive.

You stood at this window. We spoke of Tunisia, Greece, of many places. . . . In the languid afternoon.

Tenuous, fragmented, attenuated thoughts.

Tell me once more.

Start with when you bought the aquarium.

Listening to the later Schubert one pictures an old, very wise, very sad man, and he was all of that, though only thirty-one at the time of his death. I see him portly, balding—eighty-five—not so.

Let me know if you are going.

I have already lived longer than Schubert. Think of that. Sometimes a little perspective is helpful.

And how it was irresistible to him even then, that brief modulation to a remote key—

Aldo

The second episode is concerned with developments of the main theme, which eventually returns to the wrong key before floating quietly back to the tonic.

The new kitten, Salome, sees itself for the first time in the full-length mirror and is alarmed, then confused, then charmed.

You are a hopeless romantic, Ava Klein—Schubert and the cats.

A chorus of boys.

The kitten, Salome, quiet finally, in angel hours.

You are a rare and molting bird.

Danilo's recurrent dream: that his books would just go out of print, not be there anymore, disappear.

I understand that even better now.

I make no apologies.

It's Wednesday here. Edith Piaf is singing. It always reminds me of you.

Press close.

He grew old roses.

The smell of almonds and apricots. Of orange and lemon groves.

I remember Francesco, our unstoppable bodies, our optimism.

I wrote you one hundred love letters, at least.

Configurations of love, bitterness, and roses.

Bright bunches of gladiolas in shopping carts on Fourteenth Street.

Salsa floats down from a high-up apartment.

Their bellies which are vermillion. And the word *vermillion.*

She finds herself on a foreign coast on her thirty-third birthday.

And the way he stood there without speaking.

The poem demands the demise of the poet who writes it and the birth of the poet who reads it.

. . . and one of the things is science.

I'm reminded of Percival Lowell who by deduction discovered and located the planet Pluto, but died shortly before it was sighted.

We dressed as the planets and twirled.

I'm reminded of Percival Lowell picturing Pluto when thinking of my school pal Bernard Goldberg, M.D., who worked toward the cure for his own disease—imagined it precisely, vividly, but died before he could save himself.

Look, even the nuns are going swimming, Francesco says.

Because it disappears. Is disappearing. Some notes: I was quite burned by the sun. We took the overnight train. A beautiful, passing landscape imagined in the dark.

Don't be so afraid.

Look, even the nuns are going for a swim.

Years ago.

In between waves and heat, a conversation, bits of a conversation carried to me on the air. . . . If I did not care about making this a better world. . . .

. . . look at those trees. . . .

I'm thinking one of the things we should be paying attention to. . . .

She's feeling a bit better. . . .

And one of the things is science. . . .

They pass in front of me. An older man in a baseball cap, a young girl. Walking down the beach.

. . . we're meeting them at eight.

Chicken grilled over an open fire.

Ana Julia dreamt many nights of the white ox.

Mardi Gras. The farewell to flesh. I dressed in feathers. Pointed beak and glitter. How we danced, through lights and confetti. The good-bye to the body.

Not forever, but for now.

The shape of the breast against the sea in Nice.

Good-bye.

We would swing in the garden.

The path of her gaze.

The path of your gaze, Marie-Claude.

Beckett in a tree: To be an artist is to fail, as no other dares fail. That failure is his world and to shrink from it is desertion, arts and crafts, good housekeeping. . . .

Do you remember the day I threw myself in the Rhône? You fished me out. My clothes dried in the sun. . . .

Tell him that you saw us.

I had recently published an essay on contemporary American fiction entitled "Good Housekeeping."

Not exactly a popular piece.

He liked to imagine humanity migrating from star to star on vessels with huge sails driven by stellar light. . . .

This is the way to go.

A persistent dream of weightlessness.

Primo Levi, envious of astronauts.

These stories are for you, Marie-Claude, who, after the earth and its creatures, loves nothing more than the future.

[67]

Primo Levi, floating.

She taught women to drive motorcycles in the war.

Always a terrible restlessness.

Rain and *L'Avventura* in the Manhattan afternoon.

Francesco, I am dying maybe.

La Dolce Vita. La Strada.

8½.

Fill my eyes with images enough to last.

Monica Vitti on the rocks.

Fill my eyes—

The couchette and

Trees that looked like other things.

She had noticed that they had moved the wars to strange places.
Places of unimaginable lushness and heat—the jungle—or the lunar
landscapes of the desert. Places that do not seem real to Americans.
Once soldiers carrying guns, grenades, bombs, trampled delicate
flowers, dappled grasses.

A little something for the pain—

Let me know—

The sign that says bicyclettes,

And wheat being scythed all night

I am dying maybe.

Dreams of crickets.

Ava Klein, you are dreaming.

Anatole.

No, to answer your question. To have done nothing at all extraordinary to get this extraordinary disease.

You just played the odds, as if there was a choice.

We would like to study you.

Nothing unusual. There was an early desire to become an opera singer. Training in Europe.

Many years a teacher of comparative literature.

Three husbands.

Three husbands?

I wrote you one thousand love letters.

Always a restlessness.

What could she not ask of him, and therefore never get?

He sends turbans.

Our drinking and our promiscuity were just too much, perhaps, in the end. Still the best of friends.

I need to be alone.

Ava Klein, why must you ruin everything?

And always very tenderly.

Each year forty thousand people vanish into thin air. They could fill a stadium.

The couchette. . . .

I need to be alone. A strange refrain given my track record.

Three husbands.

Uncountable lovers. All unforgotten. All cherished.

Someone has brought a bonsai to this white room.

Danilo!

Avec tendresse.

Tenderly, yes.

I wrote you ten thousand love letters.

You probably never got them all.

A most unusual book.

Where are my students?

Dear Professor Klein,

Hey, how was your summer? I did the Chicago thing at the publishing corporation I told you about, and think I have become "aggressively urban" as a result. Cool experiences with city theater, politics and not an all-bad job. Some friends and I started a snazzy, underground news monthly up there as well—

I might turn the corner and there will be Cha-Cha Fernández walking his Doberman pinscher.

Or Carlos and Ana Julia in a boat.

And there's Danilo, feeling mortal again, slipping his hand under my hospital gown to touch my breast.

I remember the way she covered her mouth with her hand. Seventy now. Beautiful, flirtatious, when I bring up his name—like a young girl.

Matisse.

Matisse gazing at her living flesh as I gaze now.

You are beautiful, still.

Oh, to be in France, Marie-Claude and Emma, with you. Delphine would call and we would pile into the Citroën. She's making something tonight with champignons, Marie-Claude's favorite.

What might have been.

Someone has brought you all to this white room.

Invariably, the city is not what it used to be. It is not in 1990 what it was in 1970. And in '70 it was not like it was in '55 and so on and so on. . . . This makes little difference to the person who has just arrived from college or the farm or wherever. Two suitcases in hand, all hope.

He remembers the city of P with longing.

In the city of P, his mother made meat pies.

Delphine, who once modeled for Matisse, now a sculptor in her own right.

Maria Regina slicing a peach in the white kitchen.

Preparing the meat for braciole. Laying the pasta for ravioli to dry on the bed.

In the country she made proscuitto. Cured olives.

All that was delirious and perfect. And how swept up in it all we were, Francesco: the films and choosing the music—Khachaturian's *Masquerade*.

The books read out loud to one another in our first languages.

Pavese, Calvino, Canetti. Read them again, Francesco.

When the woman disappears, you already know that her lover and her best friend will end up together, you see it coming from a mile away, and of course, in the end he will be no good, but because of the gorgeous, the startling shots, you forget for a moment the melodrama of the plot.

The quintessential Italian male at the center.

What's wrong with this film?

OK. Enough. Basta! Francesco bellows.

Did my intelligence diminish my beauty in your eyes—my desirability?

I make no apologies.

Sleeplessness. Bad dreams: a little tree in a dish.

Ana Julia: You're the same age as Christ now.

He was sure the building was on fire, and ran stark naked holding a suitcase containing his notebooks onto Fifteenth Street where he was promptly arrested. For acting swiftly and with good sense in an emergency there were days of complications, fees.

My Aunt Sophie pleading in front of the great pit for her life.

The child babbling—the sleeping child talks jibberish.

. . . teepee.

Lights of cars across the bedroom wall. I'm afraid.

To be small in the city.

When you and I came here twelve years ago, you were already giving geography lessons.

In a geography book I fell in love with the world.

What do you want, Ava Klein?

I thought I might put some peonies along the back.

They're always nice to cut for the house, aren't they?

Dear Ava, it was heaven to talk as we did!

We felt unreasonably lucky then.

Neither Francesco nor I could be faithful to one another for more than a month or two at a time. We had, shall we say, met our matches. I was only twenty then.

We were truthful at any rate.

I was not looking for anything, anyone else, I was simply sampling.

As for Francesco? Who can say?

We were always, at any rate, truthful. Had strict rules which we stuck to:

No lovers in the apartment.

No lies.

The apartment vestibule was OK, though.

Two Germanys become one.

Regardless of the odds.

Music was everything.

A choir of archangels. I sang in the choir. Because music was every-thing then. I sang all the great choral music, because as they told me, *Christ is risen.*

Two Germanys become one. In a graveyard in France Jewish skel-etons are dug up and hung to blow in the breeze. Putting these two sentences next to each other as I have doesn't necessarily mean anything.

The request for an *indefinite leave of absence* from Hunter College granted with regret and best wishes for a "speedy recovery."

"A happy New Year."
"A bon appétit."
"A das vidanya."
"A votre santé."

Retired at thirty-nine.

So much passion in one tiny apartment vestibule. It became some-thing of an erotic imperative: an apartment vestibule, whenever possible.

Tile floors. A strange kind of light.

A bonne chance.

Comparative literature.

Still there are so many more places. I feel I have really only just begun.

I was on my way to Austria, to Germany. To walk where Ingeborg Bachmann walked. And my family once.

Ana Julia in her hammock whispers in my ear, You can forget about the diets. Because you can't imagine how much a dead woman weighs.

A bon voyage.

A remote chorus of boys.

Francesco, Anatole, Carlos. Danilo. Franz. Many others. And not to forget Bernard Reznikoff, my first love.

The intolerable sweetness of that jasmine tree in Ana Julia's backyard.

And Ana Julia—she's swatting the air.

But it is not, as you know, that summer anymore.

He had nothing left in his hand but tears, Danilo said.

Tell me another story now.

Café Loup: 234 West Thirteenth Street. And nearby, Les Trois Cochons.

In the village where Anatole lived: Marie-Claude and Emma. Our friendship surviving that marriage. Surviving Anatole.

It was a place I kept returning to.

Marie-Claude and Emma. Ana Julia, Maria Regina.

When perhaps all along what I have really wanted most is the friendship, the love of women.

You are ravishing.

Enchanting night.

Ana Julia stares at me on my wedding day. In a native gown. The dress she wore. You're the same age as Christ now.

Will night ever come?

She finds herself on her thirty-third birthday on a foreign coast.

The *Tentation* is the modern world's first statement of its direction-lessness, of its loss of coordinates, of its proliferating choices and versions of reality.

Will it finally be revealed?

A pregnant woman weeps. She was my sister.

You can't believe the fruit here. Come soon

Did you dance?

Márquez remembers: In Comodora Rivadavia, in the extreme south of Argentina, winds from the South Pole swept a whole circus away and the next day fishermen caught the bodies of giraffes and lions in their nets.

Without music, as the piece has been choreographed, the dance is even more difficult and rigorous.

What is the reason for your trip to Germany?

Are there any sorts of people based on race, religion, etc., that you would not date?

My parents singing the world into existence for themselves.

Prolonging the world with song.

Golden gown of morning.

So you can say without Schubert and Mozart, without Brahms and without Wagner, I would never have lived.

Rare blood disease,

And the silence at the end of the receiver we dance to.

There is a virus in Danilo's computer and we must go to Berlin for the antidote.

Really? Berlin.

Yes, Berlin. And perhaps Poland.

I'll meet you there.

What is the reason for your trip to Germany?

A rare computer virus.

Each ancestor, Chatwin says, while traveling through the country, was thought to have scattered a trail of words and musical notes along the line of footprints, and these dreaming tracks lay over the land as ways of communication.

The voice of my Aunt Sophie.

So many tracks the land is black.

The voice of my Uncle Solly.

Father cradling a cello. He grew old roses.

Dark music.

Beautiful fish.

And Maria Regina who lost her favorite son. And I who lost

My parents holding playing cards in the dark. Black music of hearts and clubs.

Die Zauberflöte. The last year of his life.

And I who lost—

Danilo recalls, in a Provincetown studio at night, a full moon in the window, the old poet and wise man saying "Ron Darling" with delight, as the poor, desperate, aspiring writers sat around watching the World Series with him.

Danilo now writing into smaller and smaller notebooks. Not really, I don't think, such a good sign.

In the beloved city of P.

Do you remember how the air smelled?

She trembles through thunderstorms—a grown woman.

Behemoth is danced in silence, and while it is a silence full of rhythms, the rhythms break off abruptly or disappear in long pauses.

And your pathological fear of illness, Francesco. But illness is just another lover, really.

Another country.

What is this curious lack of depression? This lack of fear? This buoyancy? This free sailing, all of a sudden?

A certain restlessness.

What is this improbable, this unlikely lightness? This fluency? I am unburdened, dying, free.

I think of those dancers and how hard they listened to hear the music that is silence.

An aquarium.

The child born after her mother's tubes were tied, named Milagro —grown now—walking with the man called Whistle at the head of the procession.

That we had any of it—it was a kind of miracle.

And the girl named Miracle—Milagro, weeping, laughing with Ana Julia, singing songs.

There's a Polaroid of Linda, the woman who was in the next bed, holding a lit jack-o'-lantern.

A toothy grin.

We just took our chances.

Danilo says that at first Havel on *MacNeil/Lehrer* looked like he was going to wet his pants he was so nervous, and now—*three months later*—he's acting like JFK.

Often, in his odd way, Danilo makes me laugh.

We just took our chances, as if we had a choice.

One wishes not to draw the obvious conclusions. Linda disappeared one morning, her bed changed and waiting for someone new.

A quote from Virginia Woolf then. To help me now: For she was a child, throwing bread to the ducks, between her parents, and at the same time a grown woman coming to her parents who stood by the lake, holding her life in her arms which, as she neared them, grew larger and larger in her arms, until it became a whole life, which she put down by them and said, "This is what I have made of it! This!"

Not another transfusion.

My parents and I walking in the American autumn, happy.

Another transfusion then.

A mahogany of leaves.

Schubert gets up having left the symphony unfinished.

Unfinished forever. And finally named that.

I might look out the window and see a stray bullet hit a young district attorney in the head.

Or a dancing Bolivian teenager in Queens, struck so hard by a passing car it knocks the shoes from her feet.

The most violent August on record. Ever.

Nuclear winter.

Prague spring.

In any other major American or European city for that matter, it is safer.

Summer in New York.

No, I am a Pisces.

Everything unsafe here.

I forget for a moment the melodrama of my own plot. This unprepared for, unseen snag. A rare blood disease.

Live, he says, more to the nurses than directly to me.

The beautiful woman I could not keep my eyes off of, waltzes into the kitchen, taking the lid from the pot and says, I'm ravishing.

Yes, you are that, I wanted to say, but did not.

Roma.

I mean—what is the word—famished, starving, ravenous— She laughs.

You are ravishing.

Blushing, staring down at my Antonioni shoes.

That was Rome in Maria Regina's kitchen, long ago.

The beautiful and hungry woman. The steam rising from the spaghetti water.

Why was it I hesitated?

Roma, for the wedding.

Barcelona for the wedding.

Roma!

Paris, for the wedding.

Prague. What would you think of Prague?

Wandering Jew that I am.

And still so much more: Russia, Africa, China, Egypt, Switzerland. And Austria.

I was on my way to Germany.

It was next on my list. . . .

Ingeborg Bachmann.

Why did I hesitate?

After a brief detour to France. Paris first. Then south.

Then Germany.

I had set out from Paris to meet the poet Francis Ponge who was living in the south.

I found his work on the lips of many of the young French bon vivants.

I loved you and Ponge.

Your lips, Anatole. Your silence. Source of all superstition, story-telling, invention, source of all mystery, for awhile.

We lost the baby, Anatole.

Green, how much I want you green, green wind, green branches....

And the line of boys sing in unison:

How often did she wait for you,
Cool face, black hair,
On this green balcony!

The young girl gathers olives in the silver-gray of the grove.

Olives hang like earrings in August, in Italy. In France. In Greece.

Green, how much I want you green.

Gray-green, blue-green, emerald.

Green, how much I want you.

Roman hills.

Francesco, how very much I want you now.

The child eats an orange. The roosters crow. And everywhere, gladiolas.

Fourteenth Street.

We knew of the risks.

I went to Spain to walk where Lorca had walked.

To ride the blue horse of his madness.

Let me know—

It was there, in the dark, after many tequilas, on the tile floor.

And Lorca—

Who would have liked Carlos, that beautiful and carefree boy.

I learned all the worst words in the language.

Lying on my back in the unbearable afternoon.

And of course, always Ana Julia.

A beautiful morning.

And I am happy for any of this. That we lived at all.

And the smoke and the saints and all the small lights we watched until morning.

Green, how much I want you.

We sat by the lake.

Green wing, green branches.

Over there, that butterfly. Quick. Quickly now.

Fleeting, momentary.

John, thirty-four, preceded in death by his companion, David.

Brad preceded by Tom. Alexander preceded by Evan. Douglas followed by Joe. George then Cliff. Arthur, Paul, Steven, Brian, Bill,

That brilliant chorus of boys.

The emblem is an upside-down champagne glass. The champagne crossed out. . . .

Bad dreams.

Without music,

He kept drawing ladders

Adieu.

Moroccan Chicken: chicken, saffron, almonds, eggs.

Reluctantly they cross the desert.

Adieu.

A moon. Two stars.

He kept drawing ladders. He hands me a pencil,

Erase the night.

Sing low in my ears.

Make a tepee. Then cross it: A

I miss the old Paris.

We were working on an erotic song cycle. It was called *Maps of the Holy Land.*

You've got a beautiful body.

It was called:

I'm glad to see you back. I thought you were gone forever.

My father hears his first English: "Don't give up the ship."

I remember the pearl sky before a storm.

We are racing toward death, Francesco. We knew it even then.

How we celebrated each holiday, each saint's day. With verve.

Touch then this moment. Caress it with your mind.

Saint Sebastian pierced by arrows. Give me your hand.

You are a rare bird.

Carlos says you are going to get sick, Ana Julia said. He saw it in a dream during the full moon. Five years ago. You can forget about the diets because you can't possibly imagine how much a dead woman weighs.

Yes he saw it, I said. But he didn't realize I was only pretending to be dead.

And by the way, he got your stolen shoes back.

Don't you think I know that—foolish girl. What could Carlos have seen in you?

Besides the obvious?

We were working on an erotic song cycle. It was called *In a Snake Garden near São Paulo*. It was called *Impressions of Africa*.

It was called *Vingt ans seule dans la forêt*.

Pierced by arrows.

Twenty Years Alone in the Forest.

It was called *La Fontaine des quatre dauphins* in Aix, Anatole, where I wept.

What I wanted to say—what I meant to say—the other night at the restaurant.

Where I looked up to the sky and wept.

Speak to me.

She's very pregnant

Orange and mimosa groves.

And under the pomegranate. . . .

García Lorca, pretending to be dead, 1927.

Danilo's daughter writes from summer camp. It is as I remember it. I hated it—hated tumbling and archery and swimming and the buddy system. I despised arts and crafts. Those stupid necklaces we made.

The word *camp* at all.

The word *chamber* at all.

Elle est charmante, n'est-ce pas? Elle est délicieuse.

I move toward you through silver-gray.

She's very pregnant.

A grove of olives.

Françoise Gilot draws a portrait of her son Claude, flying.

Claude covers the sky.

Beckett in a tree—outside Paris—the Germans below making slow circles with guns and dogs.

Artist's statement: As I was falling asleep I thought of myself painting. Maybe I was dreaming. The entrails of a dog became a ghost, then a tower, then a tree. . . . As I scraped it down to the bare bones and doused it with turpentine it occurred to me to consider the suffering of the image.

Uncle Solly in a dress.

Bad dreams.

Two children across the sky. The dead pilot pointing.

We'll go to the Pyrenees.

Wherever you like.

I've always wanted to wander in the Pyrenees.

The blind writer in the air surveys the scene.

One theory is that infected gamma globulin was used in the early '80s to treat hepatitis.

Samuel Beckett practicing the Etudes.

In the night, long ago, while I slept, he took out a small plastic bottle of water, holy water, and said, suddenly worried, Because, *if you parted . . .* darling Francesco. A baptism while I slept. Because *if you died.*

Twenty years ago.

A rare bird, even then.

Now? I say to Danilo. Not now.

But what, after all, is wrong with now?

I understand (only too well) and am forced to agree with all you say.

Beckett in Roussillon hiding in the red village for two and a half years.

I don't know why I left. I ask myself a hundred times a day. I look at myself in the mirror of the narrow cabin and seem another Federico.

Lorca in New York.

To be small in the city.

Danilo's editor carries birch bark, marshmallow leaves, elderberry flower in her purse and tells him things are going to get better at the press.

To put in your purse, Ava, powdered elm bark, beeswax, glycerin, he says tenderly.

Because what, after all, is wrong with now?

In the War Theater it is just past midnight now, in the Night Theater.

To be small. On the TV high up:

Iraq invades Kuwait. The president draws a line in the sand.

Reluctantly they cross the desert.

Neil Bush, the president's son, and his band of outlaws. The Silverado Savings and Loan Association. Hi-ho Silver.

Danilo says we Americans have forgotten how to be Americans anymore.

On Dancer, on Prancer, on Donner, on Vixen. . . .

A 200-million-dollar negligence lawsuit.

On Cupid, on Nixon. . . .

Outlaws in the promised land.

Bedtime reading: The letters of Tennessee Williams and Marie St. Just, and I have become too attached to him, and to his lover, the beloved Horse. The night that Horse finally succumbs to lung cancer in 1963, I cry like a baby. For a man already thirty-one years dead.

Hold me close.

Much of the time you are a fool, Ava Klein.

The first day of spring:

For dinner, zucchini blossoms, zucchini boats in the Provençal way.

After a few bottles of wine, after anisette, I'm laughing and saying Francesco and Ava and Angelina in a zucchini boat.

You are ravishing.

The hypnotic room at the top of the stairs. A green pulsing. A far-off lighthouse. Green light.

How much I want you.

The fertile crescent.

And Yvette Poisson dancing.

Shh—you'll wake Maria Regina. Basta!

Basil, garlic, olive oil, grated cheese. Pignoli or walnuts in the Renaissance. And in the older recipes: sheep's cheese—the local pecorino or pecorino sardo.

He was making the film *Don Juan* then.

Try to walk.

Because to love with a vengeance is our best defense.

On the flying trapeze.

I remember that night. He came from out of nowhere. We were having cocktails outside with the women. I was quite burned by the sun.

My student Daryl Moondance who gave me these purple candles that lit those boats made of zucchini.

He brings back a can of guandu from Ana Julia's kitchen.

A story without a message. He has none to give, and yet he is alive.

Thank you for the tiger lilies and the cats.

And the next morning after hours of lovemaking, he smiles: Try to walk.

Keep this.

Don du sang.

Neruda believed poetic form to be as dynamic as the processes of transformation and discovery. Form and content constantly shape each other like the elements of the ecosystem and this allows truth, infinite possibilities for expression.

You were one of the people I could least afford to lose.

And the banner in the trees reads "Don du Sang."

Passing alphabet of the morning.

Letters in the square.

Solitary, beautiful, melancholy pursuit,

To form these words

The news comes in the middle of the night, a shock, though not unexpected.

Sing low.

Beautiful lost things.

Hand and hand from the top of the Eiffel Tower.

The girl draws the letter K.

The letter L.

It is possible, apparently, to be actively dying for some time without any awareness of it. Like the people in the tornado who thought it was just another August storm.

Instructions (too late):
Go to the centermost part of the house.
Get under heavy furniture.

Or if you are in a car, get out and lie in a ditch.

Upon the remote possibility that I survive, please—

Had they said in advance that dart-throwing was a misdemeanor in the end, no big crime, maybe there would have been fewer copycats. Had they said it was only a misdemeanor, maybe the women wouldn't have been so scared. Maybe it wouldn't have hurt as much. I don't know.

We drank Five-Star Metaxa on the island of Crete, aspiring to the state of music.

Keep all this.

We were working on an erotic song cycle there. It was called *Don du Sang*.

It was going quite well.

She cried for she never would be as happy again.

A throbbing. A certain pulsing. It was going well.

Wait for us there.

A puppet theater in America. A child's version of *Richard III*. My mother weeping. Singing, a little.

The Herr Baron was going out like a light, as they say.

Five stars.

Bernard, in the hospital, was rereading *The Diary of Anne Frank*. Bewildered and pained he looks up.

I can't believe in the end—

Crucial bits of information came on the covers of matchbooks, scraps of menu, torn bits of newspapers and cigarette wrappers.

It was his aggravating habit of responding to anything I said with "c'est normal"—it's perfectly normal—even the most outrageous things I could come up with. A shrug. He's world-weary; he's heard it all—and this is nothing.

What would you say now, Anatole? Rare blood disorder.

Lie, if you can, in a ditch.

A large banner hanging in the trees: "Don du sang."

Give blood.

Two words saved their lives: Mozart. Schubert.

This music saved their lives.

I once knew a boy named Bernard Reznikoff. Quiet, carrying stacks of books, blushing. He wanted to be a doctor.

Literature and science. Gentle creature, wings on his feet.

I can't believe in the end that she just put on her coat and walked out the door.

To live close to what one feels deeply: literature or science, languages. The whitewashed wall, the fragrant myrtle, music, the fountain.

                                        Roma, 28 febbraio

Dear Ava,

Thank you for your beautiful letter. Enclosed is a little offering for you. A Purim present. I found myself going to bed with its tune in my heart and when I finally wrote it down it was so lovely that I was convinced for a few days that I had stolen it from someone; but I think not. The original recording is for boy soloist, two half-sections (four each of tenors and two of basses, clarinet, cornet and timpani). The piano reduction is adequate at least to give you an idea of how the piece goes.

Do you remember our erotic song cycle? It was performed here again just a few months ago. It strikes me still as an extraordinary collaboration.

It was called:

Let's travel while we still can.

Traipsing around the Hôtel de Ville. Trying to find a home in it all.

Let's travel.

Cape Cod light, next right. How high the tide!

Come lie with me for a moment in the room called Joie de Vivre. The light is so beautiful. And there are finches at the feeder.

In the sky a baby flying.

All those times in France we tried to donate blood and were sent away. In those days we were never sober, or sober enough.

You and me and Anais in a boat. Let's travel.

La Belle Etoile, the Azure Bar, the Café Tout Va Bien.

I kiss you one thousand times.

I was his Passionate Doll. He was my White Sheik. Francesco. . . .

The early Fellini.

On the edge of the bed—he was still writing in code. He was still not forgiving Kundera. I understand.

An intricate and beautiful code no one would publish. His third novel.

I make no apologies, Danilo says, for these texts: unorthodox but not extravagant, self-indulgent but only slightly, and refuting, I hope, all that is pretentious, misleading, and false.

I make no apologies.

I had gone to Spain to research the work of the great poet Federico García Lorca.

But what about Ingeborg Bachmann?

So much left to do.

We only live once, and rather badly.

Still . . . when the horse chestnuts are in blossom. . . .

Dearest Ava,

We have had five very full weeks here in Budapest which has included a heat wave of over 100° F.

The swimming pools are fabulous here—one goes from one spring to another, hot, cold, etc.

Still . . .

And the genêt—

Truth be told there is not one day that has gone by where I have not fallen in love with someone, with something

He takes my hand and whispers, Careful of the intercom.

Or fallen in love again.

You are a hopeless romantic, Ava Klein.

God bless Mamma and Papa, Ava, Angelina, Maria Regina, Uncle Giuseppe, Jesus your son, Mary the Immaculate Virgin, and Anna Magnani, amen.

The young Bernard Reznikoff sits next to the bed in this room and shows me an assignment he's particularly proud of. . . . Pale hands, blue eyes, a full head of curls.

He says something of the earth's gravity and of the dream life of plants. I nod and pat his hand. He holds up a book.

He holds

A mournful book.

Give me your hand.

Fallen in love—with a person, a place, an idea, a sound—

The ghost of a young boy.

We live once. And rather badly.

I can't believe in the end she just put on her coat

He whispers in my ear. He teaches me about the ancient Sumerian cosmology. Bernard, even you've come!

We were working on an erotic song cycle. It was called *The Alignment of the Planets.*

What is that mournful book?

Only the hopeless pray to Saint Jude, because if he answers your prayers he will exact a terrible price. Don't forget this, Ana Julia says.

He whispers: *Live.*

In Verona: the Adige, the amphitheater

I was retracing the great American poet's steps through Europe.

The water came up to this line, Francesco. . . .

What line? And he touches my breasts.

To there.

Yes.

The diary of a girl who had not long to live.

I went to the left and she went to the right. I was young and she was no longer young then.

The future tense we have invented and love to use.

Marie-Claude who cannot wait for the Chunnel. And all that comes next.

The disappearance of a way of life.

Bus-pas. Just like that.

My mother singing in a feather bed,

A sad and bitter song.

Ezra Pound walks along a canal in his dreamy, last madness.

Adolf Hitler pedals a tricycle.

In the hanging gardens with

He rigged up a sort of flying machine. And waterwheels. For our pleasure.

Put your feet in these straps. Flap your wings.

He was waiting for the funding for his third film to come through.

He was restless. Waiting to make the film of *Madame Butterfly*.

He was calling up his friend Franco Zeffirelli.

In his cyclist's garb. Stripes. Tight pants. You are really just a boy.

The years that followed *Madame Butterfly* were the most unhappy of his life.

In an open boat drifting out to sea.

I'm lost.

Puccini and Toscanini in the Club La Bohème.

I'm lost. Lake

Traum, come back . . . Ava Klein,

I love you still.

I am tired of overwriting, probably. A book of short stories, two
"novels," and a play in two years. They go out into the usual void
and I hear little more about them.

His obsession with rejuvenation cures.

Live.

Her face shaped like a heart.

In March Hesse wrote "sick" in large letters across her diary.

Looking for the Fountain of Youth, Ponce de León found Florida.

Marie-Claude and I, on the swing chair, imagine America.

The Fourth of July . . . the holiday called Thanksgiving. . . .

In March Puccini began jotting down sketches for *Turandot*. Find
here, it says, the characteristic, lovely, unusual melody.

Tell me more about the young lover, the very young lover who said
"star-crossed." Begin the story there.

Interrupting the search for that melody he paid a visit to the town of
Celle, the home of his remote ancestors.

What can I do to make you more comfortable?

I remember the day you invited me up to the balcony and played your favorite Mozart on the old phonograph.

You and I up there, the adagio, and time stands still.

We spoke of Barney, Stein, and Sackville-West.

I think of the thousand cups of tea that separate you from me.

That ancient olive tree in our view.

Death so near, and so far off then—

If you find my body, look for this in my shoe.

It is difficult to convey in English the exact meaning of the word *Wandern*. Perhaps "to roam" comes nearest to a definition of that half-joyous, half-melancholy notion. Wandern serves both as a symbol of freedom, of not being weighed down by responsibilities, and as a symbol of not belonging, of homelessness.

Begin the story there this time.

I'm a little lost.

No more cortisone.

On the old phonograph—Mozart.

And Schubert in their throats.

Schubert who never saw the ocean.

Who saw only the imaginary ocean.

Remember the ocean now, Ava.

Fruits of the sea.

Meerestille. Pechvogel: One pursued by ill luck. The word derives from the medieval practice of smearing branches of trees with lime or pitch to capture birds.

My songbirds.

The effects of sunlight on sexual response.

It was cold in there and it is hot out here, she babbled into the dead receiver: Aunt Sandra who survived. She was losing her mind. After all this time.

I make believe I am alive like other people. Wear a dress. Here's a little lipstick.

After all this time. Primo Levi tries to fly.

Paul Celan underwater.

I was on my way to Germany finally to

When the result of the extremely rare

Do not worry

The considerable irony of this has not been lost

Treblinka, a rather musical word.

Are you positive? Yes, I am extremely positive, Aldo said. In fact, I've got the first signs—forgetfulness, night sweats.

How can you ask me to go, without—

Most of them had long hair. What we had to do was chop off the hair. Like I mentioned, the Germans needed the hair for their purposes.

And the drowned poet says:

Black milk of daybreak we drink you at night
we drink you at noon death is a master from Germany
we drink you at sundown and in the morning we drink and we

Turning the corner the mind calls up—

Schubert, thirty-one, at his death. In the last three months of his life.

Sometimes a little perspective can be helpful.

On the other hand, Fellini turned forty on the night of the premiere of *La Dolce Vita.*

No conclusions can be drawn.

Drink this.

The essence of wandering in the wilderness.

He is on the track of Canaan all his life; it is incredible that he should see the land only when on the verge of death. This dying vision of it can only be intended to illustrate how incomplete a moment is human life, incomplete because a life like that can last forever and still be nothing but a moment. Moses fails to enter Canaan not because his life is too short, but because it is a human life.

Franz Kafka.

I was the same age as Christ that year.

Ava Klein, your chances are slim.

You remind me
of a very gentle
little girl I once
watched picking flowers.

We were working on an erotic song cycle. It was called *Flight from New York.*

Yiddish was spoken then.

A traffic jam in the desert. Trying to get to the war.

A procession of cats.

I don't think I'm seeing things.

It's a joke, darling.

Which way to the war?

The airplane is a wonderful thing, says V. S. Naipaul. You are still in one place when you arrive at the other. It is faster than the heart.

Faster than the heart. And we are back there again.

Francesco.

Bellissima, Francesco whispers.

For you, a little proscuitto di Parma.

You spoke of Trieste.

On this speeding jet toward death.

Which way to the war?

Bellissima! he shouted to me from the tower, but I just shrugged, having heard it countless, maybe twenty times that day.

Italian men saying all day long Bellissima and Che bella! and wanting never to die.

He grew red roses.

A scarlet tanager in a tree out my unlikely window. It was real. Ask Danilo.

The nurse flies by with her red cross.

I remember the Croix Rouge Française that day.

Danilo receives a new translation of ancient Sappho over the fax machine.

I took my lyre and said:

Come now, my heavenly
tortoiseshell: become
a speaking instrument.

The man to him had been a kind of mythic figure. An American adventurer. Having made his millions in Alaska, in a distant decade, having laughed heartily, charmed women, read with passion, played hard, fished. A sort of Ernest Hemingway but kinder. He never thought he'd be the type to die.

Did we not hold hands there, wiping away tears, in the snow?

They were sitting in the sitting room at the Algonquin. They were saying happy things to each other. Praise. They thought they would live forever. Their first meeting.

What are you working on now?

Danilo visits after the play. It was as if, he says, the leading actor had faxed in his performance.

The amber letters on the screen. A computer virus. No known cure.

Fax me.

Fax me harder.

A red cross on a white truck.

He had started the press because there were no books he wanted to read anymore. To City Lights—he was repaying a debt.

If we could live forever.

I never thought I'd be the type to die young, he says.

A billboard pictures Jesse Helms with the title: *Artificial Art Official.*

[102]

The billboard goes up. The billboard comes down and who can figure what's what anymore. 3M who owned the space having ordered its removal saying it was in questionable taste.

The child practices her alphabet.

Now the billboard's back. The artist speaks: I guess the 3M national executives in their central office found an old crumpled copy of the Bill of Rights buried under the papers on their desk.

The Bill of Rights. Danilo smiles, closing the paper.

Where we might have gone together, he says, I can't go alone.

And suddenly I'm closer to the end than to the beginning.

In German there are several words for horse. And there is a word for white stallion.

Did we not stand under the trade wind?

Goethe, who wrote eight lines as a young man on a wall of a mountain hut in Thuringia and where thirty-three years later he returned, refreshed the inscription, and wept.

I make no apologies.

If we could live forever. Instructions on how to:

A cup of cereal for breakfast, two slices of bread at lunch, another at dinner, with ½ cup of rice or beans or pasta. A daily maximum of 2.40 milligrams of sodium. Jam rather than butter and mustard rather than mayonnaise. Choose olive oil or canola oil over butter. Rely on fruit, ices, and sorbet for dessert or even meringues or angel-food cake.

And margarine, the spread millions use instead of butter in hopes of preventing heart disease, contains fatty acids that actually increase coronary risks.

If you had one wish.

[103]

And we learn that the cure for the computer virus may be worse than the virus itself.

A little TV high up:

Actor's Equity changed its mind today and voted to permit a white man to come to New York to re-create his portrayal of a Eurasian pimp in the hit London musical, *Miss Saigon.*

Sounds pretty awful, Danilo says.

The union, which had barred Mr. Pryce on August 7 because it could not appear to condone casting a Caucasian in the role of a Eurasian, said "it had applied an honest and moral principle in an inappropriate manner."

The first effects of people incapable of actual thinking kicks in.

Without its blue blanket of ozone—

This good earth.

The glittering sea, the sun.

Run.

Delphine, whom the aging Matisse adored. Dancing in Harlem— her favorite place in America—to jazz music.

And Anatole saying, It is normal. It's nothing, it's a lot like Pigalle. If this is Harlem I'm disappointed. I thought there would be hypodermic needles on the streets, looters, sirens, gunshots. He shrugs. I was expecting

A real Western.

An extremely rare blood disease that even Anatole would have to reluctantly admit was not, at all, in the least normal.

How rare? I ask the doctors.

I love your mouth.

Extremely.

Ava Klein, your chances are slim.

Weeks maybe?

Maybe.

Danilo quotes Nabokov: Not a single magazine has found fit to buy, or indeed to understand (and this refers also to the *New Yorker*) my last story, and as I have no intention whatever to come down to "human interest" stuff, I shall have to remain in the realm of what fools call "experimental literature" and face the consequences.

I love your breasts.

I ache.

What are my chances?

But I remember us at the Café Tout Va Bien. The Café Vivre Sa Vie.

A holiday.

Lifting a bottle of mineral water called Life in the language of the country.

We raise our glasses to the young Lorca, far away, learning to spell.

Not so far away, maybe.

You remind me of a gentle girl I once knew—

I kiss you one thousand times.

After all the dolci—the nougat, candied oranges and lemon peel, ginger and burnt almond, anisette—my sweet...after all the walnut

biscotti are through and lovemaking, Alfred Hitchcock's *Vertigo*...
what was conspiring against us, even then?

Ana Julia and the smell of burning almonds, at the end.

Grace.

Francesco telling me there is a lovely almond tablet on my tongue.
By the time it has dissolved, I am in heaven.

Stop scaring me.

Ava Klein goes to heaven?

And Francesco now making desperate promises I surely would
never have otherwise heard: *if you live—*

Find a cure.

Beloved son. Loving brother. Devoted grandson.

Cherished friend.

She speaks in a small blue voice now.

He loves roses.

On this same street they practiced arias, sang sad songs, duets,
received bitter news, laughed, wept.

Will it finally be revealed what you taught those French women
during the war, beautiful Marie-Claude?

On the swing in the summer in the south of France, we dreamt the
days away. Traditional French baby gifts: Salt for wisdom, an egg for
fecundity, bread for goodness and a matchstick.

Adieu.

We were working on an erotic song cycle. It was called *She Finds
Herself on a Foreign Coast.*

Carlos in the beveled glass.

So much yet to see:

Almost everything is yet to be written. . . .

Or see again.

They were sitting in the sitting room at the Algonquin.

Ana Julia in her winged shoes.

Dios mi amoure. Sing me to sleep.

Treblinka. A musical word, really.

In the beloved city of P. In the root cellar. And the printing press.

A painter shows slides of her work. From the earliest to the most recent. Lights out. First slide: Do you see that figure there? That's my grandmother. Second slide: There she is in the corner. And there—there's my grandmother too. The one with her back to us. Yep, that's her again. In each painting she shows us where her grandmother is. That shadow there—it's my grandma's shadow.

But one day my painting teacher said to me that I was putting my grandma into too many paintings. Next slide: A landscape. There is where my grandmother used to be. A cityscape. See up there. A seascape. Hi Grandma! A desert. The surface of the moon.

Above ground my mother hung wash.

Restoring all the buildings of Italy, Italians find this and that at every layer an angel, a lion with wings, the Madonna, and leave it all, incapable of letting anything go.

A sort of gorgeous mess.

Francesco holding on.

He has begun a film called *The War Requiem*. He is filling a room with sand.

Maria has melancholia.

I was only a child then. In the night, sirens and lights.

Wounded, shell-shocked, left for dead.

An insanity which could be passed.

Trembling in the night.

Fear.

I played in the dusty fields.

Memo: while you were out—Tomás called to say he found your manuscript moving and powerful. Magnificent. A profound delight. But he will be unable to publish it. I think those are the main points.

And now they want me to write my first book, over and over again. A book, I'd like to remind them, they never really liked in the first place.

Fears. Thunder, better than bombs.

There's nothing like bombs to take away the fear of thunder.

Fears. Danilo at night. Dreams. He dreams. Every night of thunder. And freedom.

We never found you, Aunt Sophie. Or the shoes.

Anatole in full flying regalia. But I'm not ready, Anatole.

How we celebrated each Epiphany, each Bastille Day.

I go back to earth.

I go back to earth soon. I kiss you, city of P.

Black sunflower fields.

Small horse.

Fellini's *Satyricon* in Madison Square Garden.

And the hashish, and the skyscrapers all lit, and the snow.

New York.

Where do I run?

How many francs was it to the dollar then?

A sad judgment. A melancholic one.

Human blood and seawater have identical levels of potassium, calcium, and magnesium.

I want to go there.

I want to go back there.

I want to go back there with you.

Wanderer Nachtlied

Try not to be so upset.

If you find my body, look for this in my shoe.

Eternally feminine in the eternal city.

He sends one red rose with a beautiful, sadly desperate card.

We will be there by evening.

Operatic in the afternoon.

If there is one chance in a million then it must be Ava Klein's!

The imaginary, the hypothetical one chance in a million.

He helps Fellini build a papier-mâché ship in an undulating plastic-bag ocean.

Close your eyes then.

During a seance Casanova gives Francesco sexual advice: never on your feet, never after eating.

The Piazza suggests everything. It makes me want to live—the way Mozart does and Schubert. Puccini, Verdi. Those nearly unimaginable spaces, bordered by monumental buildings. Everything here is larger than life. I know it is nearly your birthday again. Aldo, we will survive even greater sorrows than this one.

Oratorios in July.

And we walk on water for one night.

A moment of perfect grace. I offer her lavender. She crushes it under her fingers. Brings her fingers for me to smell. Tilts her head back. Laughs.

You are ravishing.

Francesco comes juggling hatboxes filled with wigs from his last film. Five hundred wigs of human hair. All black.

Madame Butterfly.

If you live. . . .

A temporary bridge of boats crosses the Giudecca Canal. Fireworks as far as the Lido. Today on the Feast of the Redeemer, third Sunday in July.

In the years 1575–76 Venice was afflicted by a great pestilence which decimated the population of the city. The Senate of the Republic of Venice decided to trust in the mercy of the Lord and made a vow to erect a new church dedicated to Christ Our Redeemer if the city was freed.

If you live—

Let me know if you are going.

Where do I run?

Father

I learned to count there.

Numbered for death.

Two Germanys become one.

We were so poor we sold our blood to pay the rent.

An apartment near the park. Lincoln Center. A job in the orchestra. Second cellist.

This temple, designed by the great architect Andrea Palladio, was inaugurated and consecrated on 27 September 1592.

Your indifferent sentence. Leveled my head.

He played the cello and wept.

At the gas chamber, when I was chosen to work there as a barber, some of the women that came in on a transport were from my town.

Did you know that Treblinka meant extermination?

No, we didn't. We just cut their hair and made them believe they were getting a nice haircut.

He asks to hear Mozart and Schubert, Wagner.

[111]

Why did I think if I loved you, I would be safe?

Because more than anything we wanted to live.

Hitler on fire. Burning like a torch. Or a last black sun.

Play me the slow movement once again.

Anatole, faire une autre chose.

Josef Schwammberger carrying sacks of gold from the mouths of victims, and jewelry.

You can fly, imagines the child. Close your eyes.

Danilo looks at me quiet on the bed. I see you are in angel hours, he says.

We danced as the planets.

You are a handful, Ava Klein.

Oratorios in July.

You apply fango to my face—Princess Borghese. From Montecatini. I love you.

And we walk on water.

These sea salts will keep the bath water warm. Put three teaspoons under hot water.

A baptism in the night.

Less of course of a handful than one time. Fifteen, twenty pounds lost in six months.

Is that right?

Run.

García Lorca, learning to spell, and not a day too soon.

Ava Klein in a beautiful black wig. Piled up high.

And I am waiting at what is suddenly this late hour, for my ship to come in—

Even if it is a papier-mâché ship on a plastic sea, after all.

We wanted to live.

How that night you rubbed "olio santo" all over me. One liter oil, chili peppers, bay leaves, rosemary.

And it's spaghetti I want at 11:00 A.M.

Maybe these cravings are a sign of pregnancy. Some late last-minute miracle. The trick of living past this life.

To devour all that is the world.

Because more than anything, we wanted to live.

Dear Bunny,

If it is quite convenient we shall come with our butterfly nets this Friday.

You will have literary texts that tolerate all kinds of freedom— unlike the more classical texts—which are not texts that delimit themselves, are not texts of territory with neat borders, with chapters, with beginnings, endings, etc., and which will be a little disquieting because you do not feel the

Border.

The edge.

How are you? I've been rereading Kleist with great enthusiasm and I wish you were around to talk to and I realize suddenly,

I miss you.

I must seem like a shadow on the bed.

I was finally on my way to Germany. When—rare blood disease—
The considerable irony of this is not wasted on me.

Aunt Sophie, looking into the ditch.

Six million.

Butterflies of every conceivable variety

Alors.

Six million, are you sure?

We were not afraid then of the dark or the cold.

City of P.

Danilo's former publishing house, Half Moon Press, has invited him
along to a "clothing optional" spa, a place many Eastern Europeans
frequent.

A nudist colony?

You will be wonderful there, I say, drifting off.

My passionate, promiscuous reading of the literature of this world.

And I realize more and more

Dvořák on the soundtrack.

Peasants worked the dirt there.

Germany, not this German Upper East Side.

A melancholy song.

Take me too.

When I awake I know it's Danilo Kiš I've slept with.

Make no apologies.

Anatole makes fun of the Americans and the thing they call "shicken." He laughs dismissively.

I smell your eau de cologne in the air. Follow the scent of you, until it is gone.

A simple game of Hide and Seek.

Bad dreams: a hill of Francesco's shoes.

Not, definitely *not* a Virgo. Not a Libra, either.

Flying into Bloomington, Illinois. A one-year teaching appointment. Long ago.

Mimi dreaming of home on the highly patterned quilt there.

Liu on the Chinese rug.

A certain homesickness.

The voluptuous and mournful music of my ancestors. The candles. The leather boxes.

Lost.

Hunter College. I need to know the size of your target disk. All day long people talked like that.

Impact me.

Run.

A student at the school: There was a war in southeast Asia. He said some of his friends' fathers died there.

Fax me a little harder.

Yes the Vietnam War. We watched it on a tiny television.

I imagined it a little differently, you said, and told your version of the Kennedy assassination. You were still unborn by a mile then.

I imagine being the bullet. He was an aspiring writer as I recall.

A particularly imaginative student.

Danilo escaping from the Russians in 1968. He was twelve.

Beloved city of P.

And his unconditional, unreasonable love of Nabokov.

On this corner where we sang songs.

How small tonight the characters from Verdi's *Aïda* look in this grand arena. And though they are gesturing passionately—how they seem to be whispering.

And the spectacle of one thousand ancient Egyptians sends the camera flashing.

A pink glow even in the evening. And then at night.

The young vendors singing over and over: beera, Coca, Fanta, Sprite.

Far off other vendors echo beera, Coca, Fanta, Sprite in elaborate counterpoint.

Verona.

Que bella! Maria Regina cries and the fireworks light up the sky. Bellissima!

That evening all streets in Prague led to the yellow opera house.

I wanted to sing the great arias with you.

We get news of a horse vaccine from China and our hopes soar.

I in my *Madame Butterfly* wig.

I know it is nearly your birthday again.

One time.

All too human, and hopeful.

We were working on an erotic song cycle. It was called:

I had wanted to see Africa. Germany. Maybe not this time.

If you come back, look for me.

They tried to force the people to undress. Most of them refused. Suddenly like a chorus they all began to sing. The whole "undressing room" rang with the Czech national anthem and the *Hatikvah.*

Anatole appears holding a book by Colette and I know something's up.

What's up? Qu'est-ce qui si passe?

Anatole, who never understood my obsession with the women writers of France. Or why his mother in the end chose, after his father's death, to live with a woman.

After the last high C, the last young lover, after breathing the air deeply like eau de cologne, after the Mozart Rondo in A. After one last ride in a zucchini boat and Beckett flying in the Joie de Vivre room, what? Then what?

Seducing Anatole into wine drinking and lovemaking early in the day.

What is this fluidity I move through?

I am a Pisces after all.

Anatole, it didn't take much. I remember. . . .

A heartbeat away.

A little Côtes du Rhône. A touch of cognac, perhaps.

Always so many hungers.

Beera, Coca, Fanta, Sprite, amen.

And we walk on water for one night.

The beautiful Margarita spinning. And how we drank margarita
after margarita in the sun.

Our incendiary year together.

The salt on your tongue.

A throbbing. A certain pulsing.

Your Picasso stance. How you liked winners and despised losers.

Carlos.

The unbelievable place the music took us.

Our salamander contentment.

Gills. The sun. Small heart.

On the Monkey River where we heard in perfect antiphony
monkeys singing.

She finds herself on a foreign coast on her thirty-third birthday.

The boat moved out of earshot. And then back into song.

And we trembled.

The way you folded the letter.

Bad news, then?

Unending fig trees.

Let me know if you are going.

Figs without end.

The air filled with oregano.

Ana Julia says amen.

The circular room began to take shape in us.

An arch in Venice.

From the sea, lavender and rose hips.

Have you brought your gazelle? the Moroccan asked Anatole. I was your gazelle, then.

A Biot jar found in Syria. A song from the beginning of time.

It's very grave, as the French like to say, I'm afraid.

How to find the arabesque?

I miss the old days.

Sunstruck, drunk, lying with lizards. Eating earth. And how you fed me flowers. And sang to me. The cock crowing, the river for a bed.

We were working on an erotic song cycle. It was called *Long Life.*

Under the pomegranate tree. Entwined in the grape arbor. Nothing and nowhere off-limits.

He calls me with clicks and hisses.

My throbbing neck, throbbing hair, throbbing fingertips. I've heard that is what happens to a woman in her mid-thirties,

She finds herself on a foreign coast.

A throbbing. A certain pulsing. She seethes.

The humiliating and stomping feet. His magnificent song of solitude—

Tragic, defiant, demented, blood-soaked in the late afternoon.

One climax after the next.

Ana Julia praying every day. Her extraordinary rosary. Round black prayers for Carlos, and this wild woman he married after two days.

She finds herself on her thirty-third birthday on a foreign coast—

Ava Klein with her peacock tail, her usual bravada.

Your visionary grandson, Ana Julia. With his mysterious grief.

We were mistaken for tortured. Left for dead. You're the same age as Christ now, Ana Julia said.

His mute violence. Savage, doomed. All along we knew it couldn't last. Wedded after a glance. In a bloodred dress.

Menosprecio de la vida.

Muchas gracias, Carlos, for coming to this room.

Your blue-black hair.

I haven't forgotten the whips. The Coca and Cinzano.

Pains in the joints.

[120]

You have a Gypsy soul, Ava Klein.

One darkened bedroom after another.

It was what you wanted sometimes. A high heel at your throat. A silk scarf in your mouth.

On the sienna tiles, on the clay earth, on the molten river, on rocks.

Deep song.

Never stop.

One open field after another. Italy. France. Or just the field in my head.

Reach.

A clearing

This is probably the last time I will write you.

Bits of remembered things: the light in your eyes.

For a moment in time we inhabited this ancient village, with its steep steps, its towers, its cats. Walked its streets. Caressed its smooth stone and columns. Heard its bells. Prayed to its saint. And the Virgin. We walked here for our allotted time—and then we were gone—barely leaving a trace.

It's OK.

We ate bread. Drank wine. We were here and though we did nothing extraordinary really, our lives still counted for something.

How beautiful we were!

It was called *Not Yet.*

In the ancient city we watched our VCRs, fucked with end-of-the-century, prophylactic abandon. We danced to beautiful rock 'n' roll music in the square. Remember?

I remember.

In the next village—

A woman wrings her wet clothes out by the river in the morning after a long night of lovemaking.

That's an almond tree. There's a cherry. Small fig.

Body oils leave the fabric. Sperm and sweat and perfume make a pretty pattern in the water. Like a fingerprint. Carried over the rocks. Good-bye.

This is probably the last time—

She says, I'm thirsty.

And the scene painter from Austria has delusions of grandeur. Nineteen-eighteen.

As I lay there it came over me that I would liberate the German people and make Germany great.

Hold me, I've got to say I'm a little afraid.

Pain. Some pain.

After everything there is to be said,

Our lives still counted for something.

Beautiful flying things.

How small tonight the characters from Verdi's opera look in this grand arena. And though they are gesturing passionately—

How they seem to be whispering

The light in your eyes.

One hundred love letters, written by hand.

And we listen to the music that is silence.

AFTERNOON

We are making our way to the Midi

Café du Midi.

In the middle of the day.

Tell him that you saw us.

We walked on enchanted land together.

Carlos doing an improvised flamenco.

Offhand, overheard, remembered things. Imaginary things.

What the story was—and if not the real story—well then, what the story was for me.

Rain and *L'Avventura* in the gray afternoon. You are beautiful.

If you find my body look for this in my shoe.

All night long they exchanged one blood for another.

And what has been left mysterious or unexplained is so because it is unknowable.

Nurses in white.

But when will we finally dance the horah?

Girl shot, three.

Maybe not this time.

A teenager who was a gunman for a crack house is charged with firing a bullet that critically wounds a three-year-old girl as she plays with her shadow on a Brooklyn sidewalk.

She was saying she was big and not to step on her.

Look in my shoe.

He paints the blue dome with clouds.

The dreaming obelisks, rotundas.

Ethyl Eichelberger, AIDS suicide, forty-five.

And there's Nabokov with a butterfly net.

Rashly he allowed his character to die before the show had reached its end, which meant that following his own script he had to remain on the floor while his colleagues continued to act. He did not stay still for long. Suddenly Ethyl offered a posthumous accordion solo. Time permitting, he might have eaten fire or cartwheeled across the stage.

It is possible to be moved by a self-portrait of 1980 in which Mapplethorpe shows himself in women's makeup, eager and girlish and almost pubescent in the frail flatness of his/her naked upper body.

Make no apologies.

Eager and girlish and almost—

I know I am lucky if music moves me in such a way—and if it has rearranged a few chaotic cells or changed the composition of my blood. . . . But even if it hasn't—still, I have been, of course, extraordinarily lucky.

A, and she repeats it: A. Letters of the alphabet. The most lovely configurations.

This is probably the last time

Let's escape this sad city a little while.

The new haircuts. What can be shaved into a human skull: clubs, hearts, herringbone, charms.

He chases me around the Roman house. A great flat-footed creature. The cats hanging on the curtains. Before spaghetti, before bed, those joyous, late afternoons.

After the hunt for fungi.

Those woods. . . .

That charming garden of cats and flowers and alabaster women, goddesses and the Virgin. And all your experiments. With wind chimes. Waterwheels. Part inventor. Madman.

Mortar and pestle

It's nice to sit here watering and watering the gardens.

And the way the swing swung.

Keep stirring the risotto.

Never stop.

Lunch.

Venice: In her glittering bowtie. Her man in the moon mask. . . .

That was me.

The pomegranate, dropping pits in luscious sticky envelopes to our laps.

Midday.

Searching for a certain lost aspect of the great poet Lorca, I found Carlos.

The Venetian blinds always closed in the blistering heat.

No, it's not possible—

All that was fluid, beautiful—

If not the bay, or the clear blue sky above it, if not blue horses, angels, then what is this fluidity I move through?

I am a Pisces, after all.

All night long they exchanged one blood for another.

Hour of death.

He dressed me in every conceivable way to suit his erotic whims. I was a shepherdess, a cardinal seated on a red cushion. A nun—of course. A young boy, of course. A woman executive from America. Francesco.

Ana Julia praying in the next room to the Virgin for a grandchild.

Flamencos. Fandangos. Deep song.

Blood-curdling screams.

Because I don't remember orgasms like that from before. My thirty-third year. A textbook case.

She finds herself on a foreign coast.

It is and is not my body.

Ava Klein, you are a textbook case.

Our child: Andalusian, Arab and Hebrew, Jew, Moor, Gypsy.

Ana Julia, amateur puppeteer and ventriloquist, puts on shows for the children with her assistants, Isabel and Milagro and Whistle.

And Carlos who wept when he first saw me because he said he had seen my death in a dream.

You are a rare bird.

A rare yet classic case.

Leave her son alone, the witch puppet says to me.

Milagro and the man named Whistle who headed Ana Julia's procession to the grave.

A little accordion solo, then?

A little posthumous accordion solo. For the end?

It's only a moment of course.

A matter of moments. This life.

As short as one of these sentences. As brief as that. But with a certain quiet beauty. As seemingly random as it all appears—there are accumulated meanings. I believe that.

Le Beaujolais Nouveau est arrivé. The third week in November. May I live until then.

And Bandol. When it is right it is a most erotic wine—with wild truffle-like aromas and a savage primordial character.

The making of pesto in Genoa is a rite and must be done with a mortar and pestle.

And at the same time,

Ten blocks away as we are lifting the most erotic wine to our lips:

A bullet shot into the air kills a twelve-year-old girl out shopping for a summer dress and sandals with her mother.

Look for this message.

Run, says the mother.

Run.

I'm already shot.

Carlos at my bedside. I wanted only calma blanca, he says. But it would never be.

A ring around the rosy.

A simple game of Hide and Seek.

Ashes.

Aida's pearl gray belly. She's in angel hours.

The sleeping child talks jibberish.

Lights of cars across the bedroom wall.

To be small in the city.

Gills.

Small heart.

No character in Beckett has ever admitted that existence is other than a cruel joke. But here in *Company* Beckett reaches into a darker dark than he has hitherto plumbed, to ask if the poor jokester didn't, after all, create us, his joke, to keep his lonely self company? This is a way of asking if in our profound and agonizing loneliness we have invented the jokester, God, to keep ourselves company?

Is there salvation for you when a film is finished?

And what is company? What have we not done for its sake? For everything human we have made up, beginning with our names. Our laws, our quaint systems of kinship, our cities, our technology, a Victorian clergyman's carefully researched study of the Sumerian cosmology—fiction all. We've made it all up, to hide a mystery in an idiotically decorated box.

Even in Genoa sometimes a little parsley. Many mix in a little butter. In Tuscany, pancetta in place of the butter, walnuts and pignoli.

The child draws the letter A.

The only reality is that we became aware of the world on our back in the dark (the womb, the cradle), with a voice speaking to us, and will end on our backs in the dark (deathbed, grave). Beckett in *Company* connects these two points of existential helplessness. We are forever on our backs in the dark, listening to a voice (dreams, the imagination, philosophy, religion, Walter Cronkite). But, as he says, the voice is company,

Or we are company for it.

Whisper in my heart, tell me you are there.

Emma remembers the fancy-dress parties.

A "la" hanging in the breeze of "va." Ça va?

I had gone in search of Colette, the great writer. 9 Rue de Beaujolais.

Not perhaps the ménage à trois he had in mind: Ava, Colette, Anatole.

And the smell of mushrooms—and apples.

Nathalie Sarraute, Hélène Cixous, Monique Wittig.

Winter roses.

Lonely, beautiful Anatole. Ashes. I was Madame Forget. For awhile.

Lost in the air in his one truly hopeful, joyful act.

Torrents of rain this August in New York.

Another time: a footprint frozen in ice.

Maybe the weather will clear.

Salt cod, Carlos, and endless oceans.

She seeks the illusion not of arriving, but of returning.

A love affair that fails.

Nostalgia. What is remembered. What never existed except as remembrance.

You were quite burned by the sun.

We've made it all up, to hide a mystery in an idiotically decorated box.

Pray for peace.

Her silk dress hugging her hips.

I heard you singing.

The plum trees.

Speaking what Anatole called my demented French.

Three slices of lemon. Three oranges. Agua mineral.

Meeting an old friend by the sea.

Is that Roger Skillings playing chess?

Coffee in the sitting room.

The various shapes love takes.

Colette on the yacht called *Eros*, remembering the "resilient determination, the will to live, the prodigious and female aptitude for happiness."

Talk of war, and then the war.

He calls himself, in his peculiar brand of English, a chump.

While we worried about hiding. And the war.

Danilo in the Red Square.

Bad dreams: He cries out. He never gets away.

Slow, halting, as I identified this or that arrondissement.

Baths and sunshine, figs, honey, sleep and walks. I was pregnant then.

After a few days of mistral, there is a blue and gold stillness so precious that I already regret it.

Older women, holding my hand, leading the way, telling me things.

Marie-Claude and Emma. Ana Julia. Maria Regina. Colette.

I was coming to meet them. In need of consolation. In need

Ingeborg Bachmann. My next project.

This is for you, Marie-Claude and Emma. Because I could not at the time get to you.

Don't count me out yet.

Do you remember the tenderness of spring here, Ava? The iris and lilac. The quince trees in flower? The horse chestnuts?

Poached pears in wine.

Already such extraordinary light.

Anatole, we lost the baby.

The mulberry tree.

You can't believe the fruit here!

The women remember. Their jewels, their loves, their griefs.

I turned and they were gone.

She wants to convey what is barely felt, never verbalized, fleeting, never arrested, common to all and developing at different states of awareness.

The flower markets, the bistros, and the sea.

Roma, 28 giugno

Dear Ava,

I've given up work on the Mass because all conductors I've spoken to here have been so discouraging. Besides I am desperately looking for a job. My biggest problem here is money. My business has failed or I have failed it and I'm trying to make my way. I've more or less been feeding myself, but the rent hasn't been paid in four months, the piano in two and the printer in six. I had a job interview to teach English to corporate clients for the *Encyclopedia Britannica* this morning. Let's hope.

I wake up. And everything has changed. Blood in a tube. A little tree in a dish.

Closeness of death.

We've invented it all.

An omelette for the first course.

Father in a funny hat. He always tried to make us laugh.

The first chestnuts in their green burrs. Half open. Three mahogany fruit.

In the beloved city of P—

I looked up and you were gone.

Aunt Sophie manic in the early morning. Her last day on earth. Scribbling and scribbling.

Like me.

I open my eyes and you have disappeared. You were a dream, Mother said.

I dreamt of a beautiful aunt.

An almond tree.

Pomegranate.

And grandparents.

A figment of the night.

I am enjoying French village life. Every day there are small denouements and epiphanies. The cherries are picked. A cow with a bell appears out of nowhere. A van selling fish arrives one day.

The Bier Belge, the umbrellas, and your pantheistic grace.

My notes on Danilo's new manuscript: an honest book—rigorous, severe on its author, rejects charm.

Significance of red?

The narrator is moving toward a single color, Danilo explains.

A remote chorus of boys—then a single boy.

Or one note.

Schubert lieder. Figments of the night. Shapes in the dark.

I can usually hear where the line is breaking.

And she always secretly loved him,

Rudolfo but—

He loves another.

My heart is breaking.

Pains.

It's time to consider learning to fly.

He later married Gisèle Le Strange, a French artist and noble-woman. Their only child, Eric, became a magician. This is my way of writing poems, he told his mother.

Colette, at eighty: I can't walk. But I try. First into your arms. Then every day over my garden. Have no fears for me. I suffer and I discover, little by little, how to lessen physical suffering.

A private paradise,

Where we order China tea and fragrant fruit, and speak,

Peonies. Perhaps some peonies along the back.

Or roses.

A circle of lemon trees cut by a cross. The cross echoed in the glass of the gazebo, in the benches, in the design of hedges.

Hundreds of fish in the pond,

Mysterious, inviting solution, like a dream.

I need days not hours in bed with you like this.

Tell me everything that you want.

We were a peace-loving people.

Despite everything.

The bullets.

The very deep longing that can never be satisfied.

Put another pillow there.

Take my ankles in your hands.

You have poetry in your soul, Ava Klein.

In the garden in Florence. Moving closer and closer to our desire. Gathered around water.

It makes me feel I might have had you honestly.

I need days like this

It mirrored everything we held dear. We danced there and dreamt, anticipating the *Rigoletto* quartet.

Just before dusk.

In the garden.

I don't think we will be asked to leave.

The broken statues said: We are ruined and beautiful, we are broken and whole.

Schubert in their throats.

Home before it was divided.

Q: What is the single most annoying comment people have made?

A: That my first novel is better than my second or third.

[137]

Home before it was divided.

We were working on an erotic song cycle. It was called *La Voix du mystère, Le Coeur du monde, The Café Pourquoi Pas.*

It was called *Les Origines du langage.*

La Fontaine de jouvence.

For Francesco on his birthday.

We were working on an erotic song cycle. It was called *The Problem of the Rose.*

One gulp and you're intoxicated.

His insistence: There is nothing that is not mysterious.

And these mysterious things, Francesco, yes, bring pleasure.

The sea, the bullet, the rose.

Ramon Fernandez, tell me, if you know—

Borges in a hot-air balloon.

The son longs for the father.

The conviction of flight, the agitation of a neighborly wind, the proximity of birds, he whispers.

Jorge Luis Borges, with his sand clock, watch, map, telescope, scale.

Show me the way there.

My mother—dressed in a gown of gold satin. Suppose it had been me?

Come quickly, she says, there are finches at the feeder.

Afternoon:

Nabokov chasing butterflies, pauses for a moment: Rahv, who had offered to print parts of my little *Lolita* in the *Partisan,* has changed his mind upon the advice of a lawyer. It depresses me to think that this pure and austere work may be treated by some flippant critic as a pornographic stunt. This danger is the more real to me since I realize *even* you neither understand nor wish to understand the texture of this intricate and unusual production.

Up close you are like a statue. . . .

I looked up and you were gone.

Where are you going?

The president draws a line in the sand.

The ancient Mesopotamian triangle.

On the teeny, tiny television: Operation Desert Shield.

Blindfold me tonight.

The Fertile Crescent.

Aldo's last hallucination: there's a floor high up in the hospital filled with pyramids and on the outside of each pyramid a list of things the dead might have done that day had they lived and

I know it is nearly your birthday again.

Borges dreams columns of numbers in chalk.

Memories of this fertile and ancient delta.

The writing starts in the left-hand margin in the strict alphabetical order of encyclopedic dictionaries. After each word is affixed the precise number of times you will see, hear, remember or live it during the course of your life.

If you find my body, look for this in my shoe.

Aunt Sophie—

The dreaming blind poet in Reykjavík touching columns of chalk.

Celebrating perfect Euclidean shapes.

On the television Gabriella Sabatini in white hitting a white ball.

The cylinder, the cube, the sphere, the pyramid.

The dream life of cities.

[April, 1944]

As Gonzalo wanted the press to seem more businesslike, more impersonal, less like a private press run by writers, we had to find an appropriate place. *The Villager* had just moved out of 17 East Thirteenth Street. It was a small, two-story house. The ground level with a cement floor was suitable for the printing press. A narrow, curved iron staircase led to the second floor, which would be perfect for the engraving press. The house rented for sixty-five dollars a month, almost twice as much as the old studio on Macdougal Street. But Gonzalo hoped it would bring him more work.

The small house was painted green. There was a large front window, big enough for displays, and it could be fixed to exhibit our beautiful books.

The Bleecker Street Cinema. The Eighth Street Bookshop.

What is this ache, deep within, for something I do not directly remember, but which was mine?

Breathe deeply. And we're there.

Time to take a little blood, Ava Klein.

In that little seaside town.

I will miss your company

Blood and seawater.

He bounded up the sea-soaked steps.

Twelve fish.

The moan of the lighthouse and roses.

Yes I remember.

Coffee is always served at the end of a dinner and it is always served black. In the north it is not accompanied by a lemon peel. It is served in another room, not at the dinner table.

Café Robusta.

You will use up the number of times assigned to you to articulate this or that hexameter and you will go on living. You will use up the number of times your heart has been assigned a heartbeat and then you will have died.

Burn oak and walnut branches. Sweep out the oven with olive branches swollen with rainwater. Maria Regina's ancient recipe for bread.

The child Borges and his father comparing encyclopedic tigers with real ones.

Word tigers—Blake's. Or Chesterton's definition: "An emblem of terrible elegance."

Thank you for the lilies.

The little girl, learning her numbers.

On the arm of her father.

Samuel Beckett alone in the dark.

When no provisions come.

Waiting.

But no provisions come.

Bone marrow transplant.

Dreams: a cone-shaped man in an infinite black and white patterned suit. He unbuttons one suit and there is another, he unbuttons that one and yes, of course, another. . . .

A crisis point.

As I write these lines, perhaps even as you read them, Robert Graves, beyond time and free of its dates and numbers is dying in Mallorca.

They call this coffee here. But I remember coffee. . . .

Spinal tap.

It could be the corner by the garden which was your paradise.

The dreaming blind poet speaks:

It could be the corner by a confectionary shop in Once, where Macedonio Fernández so fearful of death explained to us that dying is the most trivial thing that can befall us. . . .

It could be the corner by the house which Maria Kodama and I brought a wicker basket bearing a slight Abyssinian kitten that crossed the ocean.

Listen carefully.

Anatole, unfrightened on the island of El Tigre, freeing himself from the mystery that was his life. Flying.

I wanted to know the other side of the garden, Wilde told Gide in his last years.

That vague and beautiful boy. And I, the weeping Madame Forget.

Mysterious fevers. Drink this.

His invisible cities named for women.

Drink this.

City of Rachel. Marie-Claude. Monique:

The women cry out and run towards the young men arms laden with flowers which they offer them saying, Let all this have a meaning.

City of Rachel.

Singing Wagner. Dressed in black taffeta. Suppose it had been me.

He puts on a Madame Butterfly wig.

He passes out Lina Wertmüller glasses. Souvenirs from a party.

Are you sure, Ava Klein, that no one is bringing you experimental drugs? Strange blood counts. Mysterious fevers.

The president draws a line in the sand.

Strange blood counts now.

Ava, he says, live. Where we might have gone together, I can't go alone.

This is what I would like

In the end, my parents standing at the bed, singing me gently into death,

As they sang me into life,

All I can hope for.

He says, *Live*, against a pulsing field of extraordinary music.

The more you look the less certain you are of what is going on.

I am afraid there might be a war.

Memories blend. Memories fail in the end.

Pray the sound of bombs dropping does not become a kind of silence there.

I don't want them to confuse the sound of bombs dropping for silence.

A sort of white noise after awhile.

Vietnam.

Try not to worry about it now, my father says.

Yes but I feel he owes us an explanation.

I tried to stop you, but I couldn't.

Anatole, faire une autre chose.

I don't want anyone else to die.

The child Picasso who had trouble counting because he could not believe a 7 was not an upside-down nose.

Take best care,

This is probably the last time—

I came to meet Nathalie Sarraute. Monique Wittig. Hélène Cixous.

I was researching a book on the great French women writers of the twentieth century.

Anatole wanted nothing to do with it. He was unhappy even about Colette, a dead woman.

He recalls again his father in a straitjacket.

World War I fighter pilot and his beautiful child-bride, Marie-Claude.

Pray for peace.

Dear Ava Klein Guillini Forget—

I have recently been reminded of you in the most excruciating of ways—and of our one night of passion in that apartment vestibule. I might have known that just when things were behaving themselves so nicely, I would discover a new and ingenious way to torment myself. I would like to come and see you. Hopefully you will write and tell me you are married (again) and have five children or provide some other equally sane and respectable and honorable way of pointing out to me that in spite of progress made I am still and no doubt always will be completely and totally mad. (I am quite a gentle madman however—when not drinking, which as I would like to mention, I am not. . . .)

It occurs to me, Franz, that you may have been one of them.

The bullet meant for the drug kingpin instead hits—

I wonder whether he will think to look for us here.

A simple game of Hide and Seek.

A Sunday in the country.

Soupe au pistou and you.

Sundays are so peaceful here.

Franz and Danilo taking me into the darkening square.

I know a place we can still go.

We were working on an erotic song cycle. It was called *Just Before Dark in the Forbidden City.*

A presidential palace on fire.

Not hostages but guests who are not allowed to travel.

Dear Franz—

Of course I remember you. Vividly. Since we were last together I have married and divorced (you can add a Herrera if you like to my name) and am quite certain now I am going to marry one last time (Hanel). I regret having to be the bearer of bad news, but from all indications the jury is finally in: I am dying.

What odd constellation of events has brought us here?

In the circular room we danced all night to Prince. I was quite burned by the sun.

He wants simply to tell it (though not without some consideration for the people he mentions by name): his life.

What odd constellation of events

I am dying.

First star.

Borges and Coleridge wading in water.

And Schubert who never saw the sea.

The contaminated blood is taken out of the body and a bright light purifies it and then it is returned, if I have understood correctly, back to the body.

I penetrated this silent sea of meter and image which Coleridge dreamt in the last years of the century, before he saw the sea itself, which would disappoint him many years later when he went to Germany, since the sea of mere reality is less than Coleridge's platonic sea.

A seaside hotel.

Vacancy.

Little seaside star.

What is offhand, overheard, half remembered, overloved. Loved until it is a smooth stone in your palm. Bits of remembered things.

A story without a message. He has none to give and yet he is alive.

Max Frisch

Starfish.

He bounded up the sea-soaked steps.

Like Cornell, placing infinity in a box.

Everything I loved or wanted or feared is here.

Everything I cherished.

Let's put some flowers along the back.

Dear Ava,
   I began my String Quartet last year. At the time I wrote it I was listening to the quartets of Haydn, which have always amazed me with their directness, unconventional phrasing, humor and disarming use of folk music. Without aping Haydn's sound (all right, there's that all pizzicato version of the tune in my finale)

The sound of your voice. The way your letters bring you back.

It took one line.

... Also recurring are the movement's first two chords which Haydn might have well written had he lived to hear "Volare."

I am losing the vague dread.

[147]

A story without a message.

Snapdragons are always nice for a cutting garden.

The way his hair caught the light.

My father weeping. A simple game of Hide and Seek.

If you come back, look for me.

Joseph Cornell roaming around New York collecting his loot.

The planet on the table.

Your full breasts.

She sang like a bird.

The missing link. The missing clue in this elaborate treasure hunt.

My mother: Fifteen Saints in One Act.

Uncle Solly, even you've come

In a blue silk dress.

Francesco comforting his friend Francis Ford Coppola and telling reporters, He's trying to be a different Francis.

How do you want me tonight?

I believe there is a thread.

The reassurance and continuity of a thread so tenuous, so hard at times to keep hold of.

My stunned and beautiful mother.

The effects of the Treblinka death camp on one woman who survived.

A mound of flour. Dig a well. Then put eggs.

I remember your challah.

All the stars going out.

I looked up and they were gone.

Aunt Sophie screaming, tuneless, at the edge of the pit she would be shot into.

If you find my body look for this in my shoe.

Of the women, only I was spared.

If you find my body, put flowers in my hair.

And now she seems a shadow saying, Goldfinch

Holding a yellow bird in her mouth

Saying, Satin gown,

Not a person

Alabaster beauty.

In the garden now, come quickly.

An intense longing on Cornell's part to get into the box.

Consciousness flaring out of the self-contained being.

A poem written on a chocolate wrapper. His favorite kind of chocolate.

If you find this—

Trust.

Love, lie with me for a moment in the Joie de Vivre room. The light is so beautiful, and there are finches at the feeder.

So many of the old places.

Sabor. In the Village. 20 Cornelia Street. He ordered ropa vieja, and I arroz con pollo. What is remembered. And why? But I can say now

They were among the happiest days of my life.

You are a sentimental fool, Ava Klein.

I am not going to have enough time.

The futureless future.

How much I like to see you driving up—sitting very straight—in that ancient automobile.

Yes, but one can say now with what has to be called conviction *among the happiest . . . in my life.*

What is this extraordinary buoyancy?

What is this fluency?

The way we spoke—ordinary people—in letters, or at the beach, or at the moment of desire.

A white hotel room.

A solitary night.

He was very tender.

Close up you look like a statue.

He was always very tender.

I can't remember your name, anymore.

[150]

The feathery sleep of infants.

Speak.

Babies like baby talk—speech that makes use of higher-pitched sounds, melody and softened consonants. Adults for their part instinctively talk this way to babies, forming a perfectly realized evolutionary partnership.

Sing me to sleep, Mother, in perfect evolutionary—

Sing me a wordless song.

The hills were white, French blue, gray.

Let me describe my days here—

My father loved roses.

There are times when everything evaporates and we are left in a desert of pearly gray and pink and silver. I cannot tell you how enormous this vega is and this little white village in the dark poplars. At night our flesh hurts from so many stars, and we are drunk on breeze and water. I doubt that even in India there are nights so charged with fragrance, so delirious.

And the color that is the sea. In every light.

Your little-girl French. Your singsong.

We lost the baby.

Here in this small boat on the open sea.

What is this buoyancy?

And after awhile I couldn't keep track, couldn't care and you either—losing the thread of which woman when. You were sorry. Yes. We were both sorry. Me too. Very. Oh, Francesco—

Whisper in my heart. Tell me you are there.

His second novel was conceived as a memorial—

I make no apologies for its seemingly random format (it is not), its heavy dose of despair, its ludicrous idealism, or the desire on the part of the author to crawl into this elaborately decorated box.

Late one night he woke me, shivering awfully, and asked to sit on my bed. He was in the grip of panic from the sense of the vastness of space as he was becoming aware of it from studying astronomy.

We rotated on our axes. Celebrated the alignment of the planets.

This ecstatic voyaging.

Percival Lowell who sensed Pluto before his death.

Blow out the candles.

It's the swimming man.

Bad dreams.

Aldo. Swimming in the dark.

Black birds across a watery sky, drowning.

Aldo, so many bad dreams.

The night sweats had come.

Aldo, it is us, forgetful, demented a little, waving and waving from the Bridge of Sighs.

Wishing I could see pyramids, or study far things or figure out why,

Just once.

He tried to conserve moments of existence by placing them in biscuit boxes.

A blue like no other.

All too soon.

Considering everything that goes wrong—that can go wrong. It was a good life, wasn't it, for us,

Francesco?

It's obvious why everyone here is wearing crystals, amulets, the planets.

Find a cure.

A tourist from Utah, a twenty-two-year-old man is killed in the subway, protecting his mother from being attacked

And it is suddenly all too clear, that we are losing.

The bullet meant

I watched her undress,

I watched her lift her dress in the wings. She was beautiful.

You spoke of Trieste.

After the masked balls, after the jokes . . . after sex and spaghetti bolognese—we say our good-byes,

And then no more.

I think we both assumed it was something that we could bear.

I watched her lift her dress in the wings before the premiere.

Many beautiful images.

Your most perfect film.

You pushed the curls from your face. She lifted her dress. You fucked her in the wings.

We were working on an erotic song cycle. It was called *Souvenirs indiscrets.*

I watched her lift her dress, before the premiere of your most perfect film, in the wings, for you.

In the darkened city of P. Sirens.

Is Danilo then my final lover? Have I saved with some purpose his sad and hopeful country for last?

We were planning to visit the great Danilo Kiš.

The man killed when he tried to defend his mother, who was punched, and his father who was cut.

Twenty-two.

We are losing.

I'd like to try and live, somehow.

Ava Klein, thirty-nine.

I am a Pisces. Since birth.

The violent summer of 1990. Two thousand murders already

The magazine says 59 percent of New Yorkers would like to be ex-New Yorkers.

Yes, perhaps in summer.

The DJ says, "It's cloudy and dirty and dangerous and the temperature is 68 at 6:00 A.M."

Because his mother was punched.

But there is no joy, can be no joy, without acknowledgment of all the things that can go terribly wrong.

The bullet ricochets.

We would like to study you, Ava Klein. Do a few tests.

In the case of the hopeless—the effects of music.

The desperately ill.

Wolfgang was in love with his *Die Zauberflöte*. He loved it as he loved *Figaro*, with his whole heart.

The careless God-child Mozart.

Who gave me life.

Continues to give me life.

I watched her undress over and over.

In the dark.

In the German forest.

For them.

Over and over she sang a beautiful song. While my father looked on.

The wind taking away their sounds,

And dropping them in Samuel Beckett's ear who is

Waiting

Alice Toklas said yes, it was indeed true that one's knees really did knock together as described in poetry and prose.

The desperately ill. And war.

Music—the love of my mother's life.

And then: her life.

Men have skin, but women have flesh—flesh that takes and gives light,

Says Natalie Barney.

And Natalie Barney knows.

And sometimes my father was forced to play the cello while she—

Undressed.

And wept.

She speaks in a small blue voice now.

Not in words.

He loves roses.

Such a small blue voice.

Who could resist?

Such a lovely woman—girl. Fifteen years old.

She tried to hide in the woods with the boy Philip.

She remembers his hair catching the light.

It occurs to me that you might have been one of them.

En plein air.

They made him watch. He was already, by then, hopelessly in love.

She concentrated on how his hair caught the light.

Anatole's father, shell-shocked in pajamas having fallen, somehow, out of his couchette, wanders aimlessly in the small village.

Anatole flying along the blue edges of the room.

It's Sunday. I'm listening to Charles Aznavour. It always reminds me of you.

True, I am in pajamas. But that does not prevent me from being the president of France.

Marie-Claude recounts, swinging back and forth and back and forth on the swing chair.

Recalling her husband, brave pilot in the Great War.

Beau-père. Born to mad, vanquished, imaginary aristocracy.

I have not forgotten the marzipan, Marie-Claude, or the pressed violets.

Anatole's father, president of France, wandering from the delegation to embrace a tree.

Beautiful Marie-Claude, and her British lover Emma.

I remember the beautiful and strange gardens of Florence.

The effects of shelling on the French soldier during World War I.

He strolled into the lake fully clothed.

The garden in Verona.

And the tomb of Mary Magdalene—where we carved our names Ava et Anatole, and drew a heart.

He wore a bowler hat.

She was thirty-five years younger than he was. As Marie-Claude says, A marriage of inconvenience.

You have no idea what it's like to see your father in a straitjacket.

Ghostly zeppelins drifted over the Seine then, bearing their ghastly cargoes.

Let me know if you are going—

We ran to the wine cellars. Or the métro.

Alice Toklas said yes, it was indeed true.

The first time a flimsy cratelike Gotha aircraft flew over the Rue St.-Honoré, an antique dealer wearing a spiked helmet from the Franco-Prussian War fired his hunting rifle at the interloper.

A pregnant woman weeps. She was my sister.

Danilo's brother calls to say he has opened a new artists' space in Prague. Part exhibition bunker, part nightclub in a former bomb shelter. "We are calling it the Totalitarian Zone."

He brings me an aquarium. He fills it with small black fish.

Meanwhile Uncle Solly steps into the most exquisite

A beautiful boy.

Treblinka.

Open your mouth

Soon it was clear that the moon
was a horse's skull
and the air, a dark apple.

She was beautiful.

Not to have known one's mother—when she was right there.

The poet in New York on eight occasions speaks of his assassination.

Danger is near.

Pointed cactus that we bled by. Stop. Never stop.

Somehow, Carlos, you always knew.

Your conviction to live. To bleed. To sing.

Because all along—

Open your hand.

Beckett plays dirges on the flute at late hours. Joyce's "melancholy Jesus."

Ezra Pound, tireless fund-raiser: "You must help Joyce."

And Gertrude Stein in a new motorcar. Eating chocolates. And chain-smoking. "It is not so much what France gave us. But what it did not take away."

What are you all doing here?

No, stay.

What are you writing now? I have read (or rather re-read) *What Maisie Knew*. It is terrible. Perhaps there is some *other* Henry James and I am continuously hitting upon the wrong one? Danilo laughs, quoting Nabokov.

The usual American hijinks. Scott and Zelda. Bunny Wilson, Hemingway.

Where have my students gone?

Are there any questions?

Feminine can be read as the living, as something that continues to escape all boundaries, that cannot be pinned down, controlled or even conceptualized.

Cannot be arrested, and which remains—

Elusive.

What I meant to say the other night in the restaurant—

I don't know how we could have hesitated. How we could have even dreamed of hesitating given what we already knew.

One gulp, and you're intoxicated. One touch.

We were working on an erotic song cycle. It was called *Painting Gertrude's Head.*

It was called *Amelia Earhart in the Air.*

Because all along I have just wanted—

Primo Levi poised at the top of the stairs.

I have come to die with you, Erik Satie in the air-raid shelter, dressed in funeral garb, announces.

Of Ravel, Satie said: Monsieur Ravel has refused the Légion d'honneur, but his music accepts it.

Samuel Beckett was content to stay home and play Chopin on the piano. He practiced the Etudes with such fervor and dedication that his friends asked him jokingly if he was preparing for a recital.

He proposed to me at the Café Pourquoi Pas and so I said, Of course, why not?

At the Café Bien Sûr.

I was there to continue my work on Sarraute, Duras, Wittig, Cixous. This made him nervous and we were married.

And to meet the great Francis Ponge, if time permitted.

Time permitting.

Do you remember? We sat by the lake. We ate bitter chocolate. We liked to go to the park. You did your funny dance.

What I meant to say—

His love, like Sarraute for the wordless event, the tropism.

I was a good teacher, once.

Professor of comparative literature.

The imperceptible of the text, the unconscious dimension that escapes the writer, the reader.

Confetti.

My students and I celebrating the death of plot. For one thing.

In an owl's mask.

He had nightmares of Wittig's armies of women declaring war on him—his language, his culture, his body—in short, his life.

Trust me, a little.

It's taken so long.

You should have ended the book there, Danilo, with all of them up on the scaffold, whispered Dr. Day, the wizened classics professor, his mentor for years.

That should have been a clue to me, Danilo said, that he did not have long to live.

Preparing for a recital?

At the very least, I am not going to surprise you.

But when I'm better. I had the plan of going with my Danilo in search of the great Danilo Kiš.

So many plans. Time permitting.

I don't know how we could have hesitated.

Yes, but I'm afraid, Danilo says, that the great Danilo Kiš is dead.

The connotations and allusions that invisibly link stanzas and lines give silence a crucial part in the structure of the poem—

Doucement.

It's taken so long to get here.

And doesn't it feel exactly like flying?

I wrote you ten thousand love letters.

What is this melancholy melody I have tried my whole life to keep at bay?

And I still do not know what would make a person do that.

Aunt Sophie whose beautiful voice could not save her life.

Such beautiful voices we had, Aunt Sophie.

We have.

When you find my body. . . .

I know a place brighter than a million suns.

The lepidopterist tiptoes toward the unknown species.

A tiny hand carefully draws the letter A.

You spread your wings and try to fly.

They sing a bitter and astonishing song.

Her throat trembles.

I can't believe your wingspan!

What we've embraced.

And what is still left, even after everything—after many things are taken away.

I hear a thousand birds singing.

I hear you singing

A feminine text.

Mother.

The garden glitters.

The ideal, or the dream, would be to arrive at a language that heals as much as it separates. Could one imagine a language sufficiently transparent, sufficiently supple, intense, faithful so that there would be reparation and not only separation?

Even you've come!

The ultimate trust. To let go in the dark.

This undeniably dark room where I slowly unbutton—

There's a child who says: You can fly.

To speak in a language that heals as much as it separates.

I need days, not hours, like this with you.

K. Try it again: K. K.

This dark and joyful room.

January 21. Twenty years ago. And who was I then?

Slowly draw flour into the well.

We have never seen you, and we miss you.

You are a butterfly.

I feel my light dying.

I was looking for Monique Wittig. In the big cities, in the small towns, in the fields, as I had heard she was a nature lover. But she was teaching, it would turn out, in a small, prestigious college for women in the American northeast. Merde!

Lothar and Hans-Dietrich sign a treaty. Only peace, they say, will emanate from German soil.

And to the Jewish people: We are sorry for what we have done.

Trying to heal.

The longing of the dog to be a horse.

Gorbachev: We have drawn a line under World War II and we have started keeping the time of a new age.

Some pain.

The classic tragedy of my situation made us slightly uncomfortable.

The patness, not to mention considerable irony.

The parents now being asked once more to survive

Not again.

Yes.

Try not, if you can to relate it to that.

In the French cemetery Jewish graves dug up in the night.

Skeletons. Swastikas

The skeletons hung up and asked—

Please stop.

To die again.

The German nations promise it will limit the size of its army, will not acquire nuclear, chemical or biological weapons: promise that its definitive borders will consist of what are now East and West Germany

And nothing more.

And the German president is crying and saying thank you U.S. of A. for standing by us all these forty years. And James Baker is looking worried and bewildered and waiting for the translation.

Song of the Unborn Child

You have left me on the flower
Of the water's dark sobs!
The weeping I learned
will grow old,
trailing its bustle
Of sighs and tears.
Without arms, how can I push open
the door of the light?
Some other child has used them
to row his little boat.

I am afraid of the desert—known for its mirages. And without dunes—

Homicides up 29 percent

Have always been afraid.

They were speaking loudly and in German.

They were instructing her on where to stand.

Move your hand slowly like this. A little faster.

Right there.

She sees the last corner of sky vanishing forever.

Right there.

It was important to me that I be here.

She was saying she was big and not to step on her.

You spoke of Trieste.

A lament is audible from the temple and Radames tries vainly to move the stone that separates them from life.

Tutto è finito—

A line of men surrendering in desert. I feel you owe us an explanation.

Ring around a rosy, a pocket full of posies. Ashes—my heart

Look for this in my shoe.

A love letter. A path to you.

She's in angel hours.

My heart is breaking.

And you find the most beautiful woman in the world—again.

And are gone.

After awhile age disqualified us from each other, as we chose younger and younger lovers in a sort of joyful cynicism. You were looking for the way I was once, the age I was when we first met.

I wrote you ten thousand love letters.

You probably never got them all.

The dream house called Heyward in a New England of crimsons and oranges. Having returned to my country for the fall that year. Having been far from home for a long time.

A walk in the woods with my parents.

Fires in the fireplace. Every day. Every night.

We took long walks. There were—lanterns—jack-o'-lanterns. White sheets, black pointy hats, fake noses, smudged faces, cats. Crackling leaves.

These slightly dangerous woods.

We're a little lost here.

He grew old roses. She sang like a bird. Her hair—like gold.

A penny apiece.

May beetle fly
Father is at war
Mother is in Pomerania
And Pomerania is burned down.

Sometimes, we're a little scared.

The bread in braids.

A walk in the woods.

Each movement of the Brahms Third ends softly—

Whisper in my heart. Tell me you are there.

A children's song. From the Thirty Years' War. And she sings.
Finally, my mother she sings:

Without arms how can I push open—

A line in the desert.

All the stars going out.

Pain. Some pain. Ashes,

In a small town in Italy, a workman cradles—

You will always find us home between noon and three—the lunch
hour.

In the Piazza Quirinal in Rome. . . .

I've got something they're calling "bad news" and I notice I want
you to know first

At Amalfi. . . .

We celebrated each holiday, each saint's day, our birthdays.

She balances vials of blood. Strange cocktails. Drink this.

Dark and then light and then dark again. Strange. White shoes.
Along the cold floors. But are visiting hours over already? Time for
another—

Cocktail.

Making love on the red tile floors in the heat.

It's still early.

Tell me what time of day it was. And what the weather was like. . . .

The flying man takes my hand.

I'd like very much if we could talk alone.

Upon the remote possibility—

The black man moves his son to upstate New York. "I want him to live to go to high school," he says. Yes, of course.

There were many things I loved about my city.

I got your message, thank you.

And now the Bleecker Street Cinema closed.

He talks to me of this latest project. He needs ten lofts filled with sand.

Do you mean you need a desert?

A one-man show.

Francesco, it made me think we might have worked it out.

Late August and already the tomatoes almost gone here. And you brooding at the length of the growing season.

Homesick.

Baskets of fruit, jeweled fish on a tray—

When fiction explicitly becomes the drama of explaining the world to oneself—

Where are my students? Where are my notes now?

So many questions.

Writing in a language that heals.

The length of the growing season

Beloved son. Devoted brother. Uncle. Friend.

His taste for precise, complicated sexual positions. His love of threesomes. His need for variety.

Careful of the intercom.

Black hair. Deep green eyes. The sea wall.

Also his loyalty. His generosity. His little boy dependence on the breast. His love of animals. All kinds of pets. His kindness.

And I am shocked, breathless when I see him across the room at a party

Through these dangerous woods.

Whatever one comes up with to say at these awful and forever moments—you said that.

Mortal danger.

With our torches at night out for a walk among the dark, empty villas. The south of France.

Curious, how every movement ends softly.

The lipstick called Runaway Rose.

If you had one wish.

Blow out the candles.

One hundred more days.

I thought I might put some zinnias along the back. They're awfully nice for the house.

Around people's necks, on chains, on silk cords—crosses, flowers, crystals, amulets.

Unreachable Pluto.

The dream is of a disk that radiates poison gas that will kill me and the cats, but the cats first, being smaller.

I dreamed that I saw your parents, Aldo. Louisa large. Anthony restored.

Francesco carries a small cat from across the ocean.

Learn to love the questions themselves.

The spaces between words. Between thoughts. The interval

The pressures of the tide. At night.

What's Germany like?

Surely you must somehow sense it: my heart—

What happened to us, Francesco?

Is breaking.

You seem bigger than the other times.

Learn then to love the questions.

What happened to us?

I was Saturn. You were Jupiter with your many moons. It was Venice.

He bounded up the sea-soaked steps.

The fruit on those trees lit the night.

If not fall after summer if not snow on this street where you turn now in heat remembering winter, if not eternal life—

Then what?

If not birds,

Then what are these winged hopes? Still?

One wrestles, gently, with the end.

He did a sailor's jig.

I wrote you one hundred love letters—at least.

I sent you an olive branch in the mail.

I want to live long enough to go to high school, the black boy says, and yes, one can hardly blame him

Don't give up the ship.

Francesco says: Drink this.

Potions, amulets, charms.

Drink this: Five-Star Metaxa.

I hear Greek music. Crete, where we aspired to the state of music. I see a large white ship.

A desert.

And Francesco's dear friend Theo Angelopoulos, the filmmaker, rounding the corner.

The light, the darkness and you.

Some days I am so tired I forget about you.

In the same courtyard, arsenals.

And ashes, ashes

She was famished. She was ravenous. But in her lilting Italian accent she said,

I'm ravishing. I'm ravishing.

And she was.

How could I—why did I hesitate, given all that we knew, even then?

This belated grasping of the situation in the finale.

Let me know if you are going to Central Park.

The nurse sings from her station. Let me know

Let me know if you are going, she sings, turning to take the thermometer from my mouth.

What is it, Ava? Danilo asks.

I am just saying words out loud.

If not angels, then what are these winged last hopes, last things?

Eleanor and Amelia in the air.

Eleanor Roosevelt and Amelia Earhart take a night flight together,

Forbidden by the president

On impulse after a formal dinner party, Eleanor takes the controls for a few moments having always wanted to be

Women have not made discoveries because they have been kept

from the scene—absolutely.

We were working on an erotic song cycle. It was called *Towards a Female Subject.*

Through the clearing in these exciting and dangerous woods,

Where I hear you,

Singing

A Yiddish song.

A sonata written long ago by a Mademoiselle Duval. We do not know her first name. Or the year she was born. But it is beautiful.

We were working on an erotic song cycle. It was called *Going to See the Glass Flowers.*

It was called *An Afternoon at the Isabella Stewart Gardener Museum.*

They have been kept from making discoveries.

It was called *Eleanor and Amelia in the Air.*

And there's Bantcho Bantchevsky, eighty-two, who plunged to his death from the top balcony during a performance of *Macbeth.*

Flying into Verdi's perfection.

The irresistible music of the end.

Libera me.

Turn it up.

You're exactly as I remember you.

Fly.

How is this for an ending?

This dangerous clearing.

This is not to say I have not had much good luck.

We met at the Institute of Puccini Studies in Parma. You had the most beautiful tenor voice, my friend.

Voices in the ground.

And the way you held your hand over your diaphragm.

And the way you always covered your throat.

Aldo.

They'll say Moonface. They'll say Bald Eagle.

But I'm tired now of the treatments.

It was called *Landscape with Two Graves*.

This is probably the last love letter I will ever write.

I remember when we would all go to the park. Father would do his Charlie Chaplin walk.

Tell me if it is too far for you.

How did we live then? Do you remember? Did we thank God for bread and fish? Did we sing Yiddish songs?

Yes, there would be time enough to say good-bye.

In the Joie de Vivre room. Where we lived. Listened to nightingales. Walked on enchanted land.

Always one more thing to say.

[175]

That fishing village at the top of the stairs.

Francesco and I: our promiscuity. And how it suited some interior multiplicity.

That sounds good, doesn't it? How's that for a middle?

Late afternoon.

Danilo's wish: to put back together, somehow, all that was divided. A beautiful wish, after all.

So primary is homesickness as a motive for writing fiction, so powerful the yearning to memorialize what we've lived, inhabited, been hurt by and loved—

But Danilo, how can I marry you now?

Just say the words out loud, he says.

Warsaw 1944: Czeslaw Milosz

The first movement is singing,
A free voice, filling mountains and valleys.
The first movement is joy,
But it is taken away.

Breathe.

Once she was beautiful. I think she is beautiful still.

Through these dangerous woods.

Is there some internal pattern we unknowingly follow? And repeat again and again into infinity?

Danilo sighs.

Danilo sighs with pleasure. With sadness. A certain sadness. Yes.

We live once, and rather badly.

Bury her in her blue shoes. The coco shell that once held water. Her comb. Ana Julia. I think of you.

They whispered "skeleton" as you moved around the room slowly with trick-or-treat flair. Ninety pounds.

Aldo. So much blood in the operatic afternoon.

He always had to watch that excessive sentimentality did not intrude on the musical line.

This was a small flaw.

These were small flaws.

All that was civilized, informed, intelligent, funny. I miss the old days.

He had a voice like an angel: lyrical, opulent, noble, unmannered, altogether remarkable.

How then to find the arabesque?

The struggle all along—how to accept one's inner voice.

What did I want in the end?

Dear Ava,
    If I tell you that everything's been very "interesting"—that there's been lots of "learning and growing"—you'll judge, I'm sure, the extent of my despair accurately.

I miss the old days.

They were going to go to the river.

News of your illness turns every blue day here to lead.

Mira, Ana Julia says pointing.

I tell him now to love the gray days.

Somewhere a young girl—

Over so much static.

Who was I that I thought this would be so easy?

Who was the person I thought I was?

You gave me the world.

Who will lead me there, if not you?

The poet writes: love. The poet writes: death.

Brilliant, consolatory, you take us in, dear Cathy, and your much loved husband, Harry.

Icarus falls from the sky into an Aegean so blue it must have looked like—well—paradise,

Maybe or Eleanor Roosevelt's billowing blouse.

Somewhere a young girl—

The light in her eyes.

For Cixous, female sexual pleasure constitutes a potential disturbance to the masculine order.

Swimming in the tropical sea. We ate fresh fish in beautiful boats—

We heard a blue guitar

I know a place that burns so bright, Carlos. . . .

Like a million suns.

How did I end up here again? With you? Against better judgment. Against everything? And the roses—

I sent you an olive branch in the mail.

How strange in the end.

My father. The white on his sideburns. Glowing in the night.

What I meant to say the other night at the restaurant . . . that is—is that—what I meant—

And my longing—and for what? At this late hour?

It was something I meant to say.

What do you want?

Somewhere a young girl.

In the glowing light of the moon. Your silver sideburns. Your jet black jacket.

What I meant to say the other night in the restaurant—

He loves roses.

She's got a beautiful voice.

My songbird.

The embroidered F on the handkerchief you used to wipe your semen from my face.

After sex, in the airplane bathroom and eau de toilette.

And which I kept, unwashed, for a long time. It's been years now.

I count all the airplanes I've taken, to sleep.

Try to sleep.

In the unlikely event of a power loss

I realize I am in 27E, not 27F, and I move over one. That's better. Not so symmetrical. So perfectly centered for—fasten your seat belts. We are experiencing—turbulence. Not to worry.

In that too small, too private plane—for my tastes.

But it is painfully obvious that we are not flying to France this time.

Irish faces. Italians—where am I? Boston. Not to teach, but for a *second opinion.*

Dana Farber Institute.

Dana Farber Fancy Cancer Institute.

Which is really a third or fourth opinion. Or—

Who's counting?

Danilo who takes my hand.

A sixth opinion. I love you.

High up in the air.

We pass Samuel Beckett who's hiding in a tall tree. German guard dogs below.

Ana Julia in her after-death dream flies by, hoping to catch that bandit and hold those slippers one last time.

Thirty-five thousand feet.

In the event of a power loss.

All seats can be used as rafts.

A firm tug starts the flow of oxygen.

He tries to conserve moments of existence by placing them in biscuit boxes.

I remember the full moon on the wing that took me to you.

There's Boston down there. France. There's Rome. A place I loved.

I was on my way to Germany.

Ingeborg Bachmann.

Steel and light.

I was composing an utterly beautiful line of the erotic song cycle when—

All crafts are equipped with flotation-aid devices. In some cases it will be your seat.

It feels tilted even before it goes up.

The effects of flying on sexual response.

People are going everywhere. Caracas, Brussels, Chicago. I am going to the Dana Farber Cancer Institute.

What is Zantop?

It was not my purpose to bring them so close together: Francesco, Danilo, Carlos, now Anatole.

In the Joie de Vivre room.

Great cities of the world.

Great literature of the world.

A plane with the letters on the side that say Zantop.

[181]

I was on my way to Germany.

The book yields its secret. Six million dead. For months I refuse to believe.

This is probably the last time you will hear from me.

A ring around a rosy.

How can the air hold us? I asked, pointing to a plane.

Ashes.

He was watering the roses and ashes.

Can we make holes for the air?

What I am trying to ask—

Six million people

I know this letter will probably never get to you. When you find my body—

I cannot imagine surviving anymore, as hard as that is to say.

Have you left the key in its old hiding spot?

Look for this—

In the land we were born

Just a bone and a heart

A penny apiece.

He tries to conserve moments of existence in biscuit boxes

And I wonder what would make one person do that to another

Six million times.

How we liked so much to go to the park. Father would do his funny walk that made Mother and Rachel and I laugh so hard we fell in the grass.

Name the baby for me, Sophie begs.

I want to live.

He bats his curly lashes.

Uncle Solly, it's you! I always knew I'd see you again!

A child tries to fly.

So many songbirds

And stars

Going out.

And the smoke as she speaks.

Gently now.

We made May baskets.

Picked crocuses for our favorite teacher.

Ashes in the ground.

Bernard and I late at night promising to save ourselves for music and truth and beauty and each other.

The longest night of the year.

An elevator ascending. Bernard carries my books.

There's a thin man Francesco insists can rise.

[183]

Drink this, Francesco says.

In the night he baptizes me again and again with tears and holy water from Rome, because, *if you die.*

Drink this.

A festival of lights on the year's longest night.

He bounds up, two at a time, the sea-soaked steps.

And we walk on water for one night.

Now he comes with one last acrobatic position. Raise your leg. Give me your hands. Turn this way. Yes. Close your eyes.

One more time.

Anton Chekhov crosses Siberia to Sakhalin, the remote penal colony island, to conduct a prisoner census no one wants.

God knows, wrote Chekhov in his ledger, what this young, lovely girl whom fate has brought to Sakhalin is dreaming about.

Women who were convicted of murder but were ultimately being punished for their love affairs.

Whom fate has brought here.

I admit wanting once the love of every man—not to mention the last, most complicated, most exquisite sexual position.

In a wedding dress.

Let's take it a little slower.

Today, of course, is a holiday.

Shifting voices and constant breaks of mode let silence have its share and allow for a fuller meditative field than is possible in linear narrative or analysis.

[184]

My passion for

Silly, really,

I don't want to die yet.

My desire at this moment for Mozart. For Schubert.

Part of me feels that it is superfluous—that if I need rubber to use—
that is most important. Life doesn't last, art doesn't last—

Who saved their lives,

And mine.

The child Beckett, perched in a tree, imagining that he might fly.

Light bouncing off the left wing.

She was saying she was big and not to step on her.

He thought of the glory of the clouds.

One became jealous of the other, having detected my sexual
attention to have shifted.

Silly, really, at this point.

Danilo carries a bonsai across town.

It's getting hard to stay awake.

And at last I understand how love ends.

You close your eyes.

We fed the ducks. We danced in the circular room for one night.

Fleeting, random,

You took my hand.

Careful of the intercom.

Precious, disappearing things.

A peach on a white plate.

Let me know if you are going—

My dear father who cannot bear endings of any kind. Leaving one spoonful of oatmeal in his bowl. One basil plant in the ground in winter.

And I who now cannot bear beginnings.

Not anymore.

Will you marry me?

Not now.

If not now, then when?

I love your hair. I love your breasts.

A new dress for the wedding. Music. Flowers.

A sudden shift in direction. The left wing dips.

I want you.

And yes. Why not? If not now, then when?

How was it possible I took everything for granted?

It snowed for a long time that year.

In the flatlands where

Each night I dreamt of a curvaceous woman.

She was my mother. And

She sang.

He pets me like a cat.

If you let me fly once more, I'd be the model passenger. I swear I'll buckle and unbuckle and buckle and unbuckle just as many times as you tell me. No flirting with the stewards.

Don't say it unless it's true.

No touching, no fantastic explorations with fellow passengers under blankets or winter coats on international night flights.

Blood in a cylinder.

A throbbing.

A certain pulsing.

I'd like to fuck you right here.

I know a place more brilliant than a million suns.

They would have drunk a limonada.

What is this gratitude? This reconciliation? That has caught me so off-guard?

I have seen the sea twice, first the Adriatic, then the Mediterranean, but both as it were only in passing. In Naples we shall get better acquainted. Everything in me is suddenly beginning to emerge clearly. Why not earlier? Why at such cost? I have so many thousands of things, some new, some from an earlier time, which I would like to tell you.

Goethe in Rome.

I always meant to go

How was it I got so sidetracked?

Some pain. Hard to explain.

Where? Ava Klein. Show me where now.

Hard to explain.

A certain aplomb. A certain élan. Words I love.

We were a peace-loving people.

Baskets of fruit, jeweled fish on a tray, he falls on his knees, he says *live.*

Try not to be so afraid.

We were a peace-loving people. Despite the evidence.

Tell me how and where does love end?

So no late-hour, last-minute bone marrow transplants now, please.

Passenger Klein.

The clouds today from twenty thousand feet look like a field of snow.

I hear a remote chorus of boys.

Bernard. Francesco. Anatole. Carlos. Danilo. . . .

We were working on an erotic song cycle. It was called *Preparations for Nuptials on the Other Side of the Abyss.*

Because always you were asked to give one more thing up.

Nineteen-ninety: I drag out, one more time, my feather headdress. I say it to myself: You are a rare bird, Ava Klein.

[188]

You pick an odd time to feel like a bird.

We are beginning our descent.

Passenger Klein.

Anatole, faire une autre chose.

The tilted cities.

We were capable of many kinds of love.

Sex with you, Francesco, over the phone. I have not forgotten.

My feather bed.

Your friend Francis Ford Coppola, whom you always defended even when he was indefensible, and Federico Fellini whom you love, and Bernardo Bertolucci, now filming in Morocco. . . .

And your great pasta wars.

By the time you leave the hospital the leaves will be off the trees and we'll be able to see the river better.

Danilo. As much an optimist as you are a pessimist.

It's lovely to sit in the garden.

On the dating service questionnaire: I am more a ( ) talker, ( ) listener, ( ) both.

My dear friend.

Today of course is a holiday in Poland.

Iraq invades Kuwait. The president draws a line in the sand today.

Mistakenly, children are killed.

Who besides you—to say no more—to take my hand, to pull the infamous plug if necessary.

No.

Because what, after all, is wrong with now?

You wanted once everything that I wanted.

And now for the aerobic version:

She had black hair and red lips and they called her a Gypsy and she was beautiful. He was large with a balding head and a noble profile and he wore a bowler hat and he was beautiful. There was an olive grove next to a house made of stone and all summer the sun shone and it was beautiful. And he had a mass of curling hair and wire rim glasses and wore only the most ragged of sweaters and he was beautiful. And the way he touched me in the afternoon was beautiful,

It was called *The Last Chance Saloon.*

And there were two children with voices like birds and they were my parents and they were beautiful.

And the look on the face of the man, and the pink glow coming from the triangle he wore and the way he wept was beautiful.

And his kidskin gloves.

And his black gown.

And the poems the drowned man wrote—and the songs. And the way the story surely will end is beautiful.

Black milk of daybreak we drink it at nightfall
we drink it at noon in the morning we drink it at night
drink it and drink it
we are digging a grave in the sky it is ample to lie there

I know this letter will probably never get to you.

What did she dream?

In the great pasta wars that week the subject was pesto.

In Tuscany it is made with a mezzaluna, in—

Never a mezzaluna! And never, not ever in a food processor.

We judged with our eyes closed.

I'll never understand why love does not stop.

Close your eyes, Ava Klein.

And after everything we put each other through.

Before his death Danilo's friend Harry lost his short-term memory, so he could not remember that he was broke and that his wife had left him.

He flits in wearing a tiara and sash, high heels, beautiful garter belt and stockings. Halloween long ago. The Statue of Liberty on his arm. That was me.

The dancing Limoges apple and how her hand trembled.

Reaching for the orange

Rue des Favorites.

Mistakenly the bomb hits where children lived.

On the old phonograph we played Brahms and Mozart,

Bach.

It is intellectually monstrous. You can play it backwards and upside-down and everything continues to work. Do you realize what that represents in self-control, in unlimited technique? However, the interest of these works isn't purely intellectual, because their author is an immense musician, a man who—fragile as he was, miserable as he was—had presence, a notion of the mysteries surrounding him and opened them to us and made us feel them.

Listen to the white ox inside you.

Strange dreams.

His clouded and marbled eye.

The vast sky, and Ava Klein so small.

You're like the same person, only different.

In perfect simplicity.

In synchronicity.

Thank you.

Reaching,

A little girl learns her alphabet.

Now they are testing light.

Find a cure.

In Israel archaeologists unearth a golden calf.

The tiny calf of mostly bronze recovered almost intact, with legs, ears, tail and one of its two horns still in place, even though the temple in which it was housed was destroyed during a conquest of Ashkelon in about 1550 B.C., midway through the Bronze Age.

Still, if he could reach R it would be something. Here at least was Q. He dug his heels in at Q. Q he was sure of. Q he could demonstrate. If Q then is Q—R—

The golden calf is believed to have been the central object of worship for the Canaanites for over one thousand years.

But after Q? What comes next? After Q there are a number of letters the last of which is scarcely visible to mortal eyes, but glimmers red in the distance.

He was swallowing special pills and light.

We dressed as the planets. Wore solar meteorites around our necks and charms.

R.

They kiss calf images.

And dancing.

Today, the news: a golden calf, and ultraviolet light.

Flying machines and waterwheels. Great inventions. The future tense.

Aunt Sophie dancing in a circle.

My mother singing a song that Samuel Beckett, waiting, hears across the sadness that is Europe

Elongation of the day, of the phrase

And the memory of shellfish, and the steps.

A tray of jewels. Fruits of the sea. Twelve fish. Will you marry me?

You were all I ever wanted.

She tap-danced through one of his films while telling stories of all the men in her life. One of them Francesco.

News to me.

Not fidelity, but truthfulness had been our pledge.

[193]

Now we learn that there is almost no such thing as monogamy.

You were Jupiter trailed by your many moons.

In a burst of new studies we see, biologists say, that infidelity is rampant in the animal kingdom.

I miss the old days.

And craftily faithless.

They hold mesmerizing, obliterating light in their bodies. We are hopeless and go.

Talking of—

The new research gives the lie to the old stereotype that only males are promiscuous.

A landscape of joy.

It's all baloney. And what we've found lately is only the tip of the iceberg. This is Anais's date from the dating service speaking. Philandering biologist researcher.

The black-capped chickadee.

I miss the old days.

Especially the black-capped chickadee

And barn swallows. When cheating, he says, the female invariably copulates with males endowed with slightly longer tails than those of their mates.

Consider the queen bee. And the drones who die for it. Exploding their genitals onto her body.

Nervous dating-service date of Anais.

Careful of the intercom

And the monstrous, extraordinary creatures he turned the women he loved (and some he did not) into—glowing, enormous, mythic, feathered, finned. Many-legged creatures of the sea.

Bejeweled. Bellissima! Che bella!

I love your tail.

They arrive in their ancient car.

We used to love to go to the park.

Thank you.

Tanglewood for the day.

The Berlioz *Requiem.*

A last extravagance. The *Requiem.* A last madness.

Four brass choirs.

Such a strange piece really. The mumbling half steps of the Kyrie,

What did I want from you?

The odd punctuations, the uneven phrasings of the Lacrimosa.

I hear the irresistible music of the end.

The great Lacrimosa,

The eerie two-note commentary in the Offertorium.

Aldo

I hear now the irresistible music of the end.

When all along we just wanted the same thing: to be free.

Anatole's love for all things French. Even the Berlioz *Requiem*.

Fly. He looks to the sky.

He bows his head in deep shadow. He turns gentle with one touch.

At the Café Un, Deux, Trois

Vier, fünf, sechs, sieben, acht, neun, zehn.

Where—

Ready or not, here I come.

Don't cry.

Try not to cry now.

Truffle omelettes. Snails. Lamb.

And the chicken of Bresse, sporting their patriotic medals.

Shall we take the upper or the lower corniche?

I wish you were here.

The melons of Cavaillon. Olive oil from Provence. Anchovies from Collioure. Normandy butter. Brittany oysters and Anatole, you.

How does this strike you as a beginning?

I would say, "le weekend," "le super marché." "Le super sexy weekend." You'd cover your ears and cringe.

Sans à venir.

And look to the sky.

Primo Levi stands at the top of the staircase.

No. Don't,

You are beautiful.

Do you remember the day I threw myself into the Rhône?

We were grape harvesting.

You fished me out.

That's all dead and buried

My clothes dried in the sun.

Danilo recalls the books made there: typewritten, held together by nails.

His father's books.

The tanks had not yet come.

We were working on an erotic song cycle. It was called *Forty Days and Forty Nights.*

It was called *The Darkest Evening of the Year.*

It was called:

Try Not to Be So Afraid.

It was held together by nails, and tears.

The bullet was not meant, of course, for Shaniqua, aged ten, on a shopping trip with her mother and sister in the Flatbush section of Brooklyn.

A quarrel outside a jewelry store.

Her life over.

One loses count.

One loses heart.

She made funny faces.

Her father remembers she was the only one who could make him move—get pizza, say, after a day's work.

They were shopping for shoes. It was still June then.

Just the beginning

Run.

Mommy, I've already been shot.

Whisper in my heart. Tell me you are there.

The president draws a line in sand.

It was called *Anticipation of the Night.*

I feel you owe us an explanation.

It's only thunder.

Take my hand.

X marks the spot.

There was a war on. So many stray bullets. So much poverty.

4. Sergei Nabokov (1900–1945) had, like his father, a passionate interest in music, especially Wagner, an interest his brother Vladimir could not share. He was, between the two world wars, a well-known figure in European musical and theatrical circles. According to a close Russian friend of his, Sergei Nabokov fell victim to Hitler's systematic campaign to exterminate all homosexuals.

Whisper in my heart.

Danilo sits in the last square of light. Tell me you are there.

I'm glad to see you back. I thought you were gone forever.

Francesco's friend, Mario Botta, the architect from Lugano who will design the Museum of Modern Art in San Francisco.

A brooding and crisp structure.

A classical formality

So we might be spared

Even medieval. A controlled solemnity.

The sound of bells

Sing to me

Francesco's voice sparkles over the phone. On the top: a ring of trees, a vast crown of laurels planted all around the sliced-off top of a cylinder of stone.

And the building will seem to sway.

To smile.

What did I want from you in the end, Francesco? What could I not ask for and therefore never get? My Italian was good. That was never the problem.

The tragic sense of life.

Francesco, I remember the trays of cologne. What did I want?

It is the week before Christmas. In the apartment across the way a man works on a dollhouse. So what if we are doomed? He will die rubbing a small chair smooth.

Galanos at sixty-six: All I have ever wanted is to make beautiful dresses.

A beautiful ambition, after all.

An imperial tomb is excavated. One million little men of mud found in China.

It was one of the greatest periods in Chinese history. Paper and porcelain were invented. Philosophical and historical studies flowered.

We were working on an erotic song cycle: *Roma, 28 febbraio 1990:*

Thank you for your beautiful letter. Enclosed is a little offering for you. A Purim present. . . . I found myself going to bed with its tune in my heart and when I finally wrote it down it was so lovely that I was convinced for a few days that I had stolen it from someone; but I think not. The original scoring is for boy soloist, two half sections (four each) of tenors and

All terra-cotta. All sixty-centimeters-tall naked male figures, armless, all red.

Do you remember our erotic song cycle, Andrew? It was called:

What I am really afraid of, dearest Ava, is to die with the feeling that the abundant blessings which the Lord has bestowed on me will have been wasted. I feel as though I have not fulfilled my promise or my mission. That is cruelest of all. And I am afraid of having to live with my mother out of poverty or helplessness. I wish I could find a way so that whatever meager gifts I have as an artist might feed me, keep me in the world, give me meaningful work and community. But truthfully, as with my fate with the *Requiem,* I fear that it is no longer possible, that I derailed myself somewhere back there, not willingly and somehow not even unconsciously, but stupidly, blindly ruled somehow by my excessive passion and not by what you generously call my formidable intelligence.

We dressed as planets and the stars.

I am writing, dear Ava, to tell you that I, too, have tested positive for the AIDS virus.

She dreams of the Channel Tunnel. The Chunnel. To the French, La Manche. Marie-Claude—who loves nothing more than the future.

Loving as time passed—motorcycles, airplanes, cities of glass, space travel and now this.

Find a cure

Venice 1976

I go on loving you like water.

She dreamed of flying without a machine. Delta Plan. She showed me a man with wings.

Samuel Beckett spreads his wings:

I have a great desire to get on with my work but can't get near it at the moment. I see a little clearly at last what my writing is about and fear I have perhaps ten years courage and energy to get the job done. The feeling of getting oneself in perfection is a strange one, after so many years of expression in blindness.

I step onto the Train de Grande Vitesse.

A woman. My age. Drenched. Standing over my bed. And who are you? I ask. She smiles and shrugs. I love her, whoever she is.

He is on the track of Canaan all his life; it is incredible that he should see the land only when—

How did I end up there? Drinking vieux marc again with you?

Against my desire. Against all better judgment.

They were blue and they opened up in water.

I did not think he would come here again.

After the first night he writes he is a madman and in love.

[201]

They opened up in water.

Never to have touched a woman like that.

What in the world was I waiting for? How could I have hesitated given—

This belated grasping

You are beautiful.

Blow out the candles, now.

I have a great and astonishing sense of something there, which is "it." It is not exactly beauty I mean. It is that the thing itself is enough; satisfactory; achieved. A sense of my own strangeness walking on the earth is there too: of the infinite oddity of the human position; trotting along Russell Square with the moon up there and those mountains and clouds. Who am I, what am I and so on: these questions are always finally about me; and then I bump up against some exact fact—a letter, a person, and come to them again with a great sense of freshness and so it goes on. But on this showing, which is quite true I think, I do fairly frequently come upon this "it" and then feel quite at rest.

It's taken all this time to be free.

And how you surprise yourself. How you thought you'd be willing to try anything, do anything—but now I resist this desperate, last, late hope.

No. No more chemotherapy. No more potions.

Drink this. Pretend we are at the Café Pourquoi Pas.

Will you marry me?

Maybe not right now.

Drink this.

A line of poplars in summer.

Each night I dreamt of a curvaceous woman.

She was my mother. And

She sang.

He pets me like a cat.

If you let me fly once more, I'd be the model passenger. I swear I'll buckle and unbuckle and buckle and unbuckle just as many times as you tell me. No flirting with the stewards.

Don't say it unless it's true.

No touching, no fantastic explorations with fellow passengers under blankets or winter coats on international night flights.

Blood in a cylinder.

A throbbing.

A certain pulsing.

I'd like to fuck you right here.

I know a place more brilliant than a million suns.

They would have drunk a limonada.

What is this gratitude? This reconciliation? That has caught me so off-guard?

I have seen the sea twice, first the Adriatic, then the Mediterranean, but both as it were only in passing. In Naples we shall get better acquainted. Everything in me is suddenly beginning to emerge clearly. Why not earlier? Why at such cost? I have so many thousands of things, some new, some from an earlier time, which I would like to tell you.

Goethe in Rome.

I always meant to go

How was it I got so sidetracked?

Some pain. Hard to explain.

Where? Ava Klein. Show me where now.

Hard to explain.

A certain aplomb. A certain élan. Words I love.

We were a peace-loving people.

Baskets of fruit, jeweled fish on a tray, he falls on his knees, he says
live.

Try not to be so afraid.

We were a peace-loving people. Despite the evidence.

Tell me how and where does love end?

So no late-hour, last-minute bone marrow transplants now, please.

Passenger Klein.

The clouds today from twenty thousand feet look like a field of snow.

I hear a remote chorus of boys.

Bernard. Francesco. Anatole. Carlos. Danilo. . . .

We were working on an erotic song cycle. It was called *Preparations for Nuptials on the Other Side of the Abyss.*

Because always you were asked to give one more thing up.

Nineteen-ninety: I drag out, one more time, my feather headdress. I say it to myself: You are a rare bird, Ava Klein.

You pick an odd time to feel like a bird, Ava Klein.

Across the Vltava River, deep under the square where the monument of Stalin once stood, a 108,000-square-foot bomb shelter the communists built for themselves is now Czechoslovakia's biggest gallery.

I wanted to keep you from pain.

There is pain now, Mother. But not suffering.

Sing to me.

A beautiful Yiddish melody.

She finds herself in her thirty-ninth year on a foreign coast,

Drawing the letter D in the air.

In my stationary bed. In my hospital gown.

Radiant with our deaths.

Danilo, the tanks had not yet come.

There is no subject. There is only mystery. There are only questions.

After the masked balls, after the jokes, after sex and spaghetti bolognese. After all the mad aristocrats and decaying pallazzos, after the silly plot contrivances

Deepening, enchanting night.

Dear Ava,

Yesterday in the sauna I was filled with the image of us walking in that intense thunderstorm in Verona—crossing the river, drenched in the night. The sensation came over me in the heat—so vividly.

One last glimpse.

Enough images to last.

Yvette Poisson dancing.

The teeny tiny television here where sea turtles weep as they lay
their eggs.

Pacman on a lonely black background. He knows he's not really
alone, the child says.

The pediatric wing.

He senses Fireman is near.

They were sent one way and I the other

A deepening sense of loss.

The irreplaceable Ethyl Eichelberger.

A deepening sense of musical structure.

He carries tiger lilies. Kisses my hand, says let go when you want.

A ring of mud.

Danilo.

I will.

He felt too good to lie down on the sand so went walking along the
beach, just ankle deep in the glassy water, feeling it suck away at his
feet and then flood back in, watching the patterns disappear and
change like abstract and instantaneous photographs, compositions
of water and sand, fleeting, but sharp and definite for their instance
of coherence. He was glad to be here to see them, for they would
never recur.

Where I take your hand once more in the dark.

The movie houses. The Yorktown, the Symphony, the Thalia.

Our telephone exchange: Trafalgar.

My parents recall the mezzanine.

Butterfield, Monument, Spring.

Trafalgar 1-6824

And walking from the subway at Columbus across Fifty-ninth on the park side. The Little Carnegie, the Normandie, the Victoria.

Gone, my father whispers.

The Lyric. The Apollo.

Please not now.

The assailant blew the darts through a tiny blowgun-like device into the buttocks of women.

I've forgotten your name.

What is your sign again?

Dear Ava,
    Halfway around the world in my pursuit of the Ideal Woman and/or Kathy. Hope all is well in the Apple.

Twenty-two murdered cabdrivers so far.

The Bengal tiger, solitary, nocturnal, nearly extinct.

On the teeny tiny television, way up.

At the place where dreams intersect, where the Bengal tiger and the mist—where the dusk and the cinema and blood merge—they live.

Give me your good arm.

I'm afraid my fractured wrist is healing very slowly. I am still very much a one-armed girl.

I think of you sitting on the terrace

Where I take your hand one last time

You say I am thirsty

Where I hand you a glass of water

Aldo drink. You say thank you.

Where you say, how can I thank you?

Let's samba.

Let's sing a duet.

Let's play a posthumous accordion solo together soon.

Let's samba. Let's tango. Let's do a little improvised flamenco. Right here. Right now.

Because what, after all, is wrong with now?

We had prolonged the world a little while at least with song.

In Rio at Carnaval.

A farewell to the body.

I came to celebrate. To praise.

A rare and precious bird.

Remember Mexico.

I remember Mexico.

Dance with me.

Floating out on a yacht called *Eros*. Let go. With both hands now.

Dos Equis. Five-Star Metaxa. There's a child who says: You can fly. On the Day of the Dead.

S & m—it stood for sex and magic. It was all about desire. It was all about trust.

We like to imagine that maybe there was music in the background.

His precise and relentless dreams of my death. How could we survive that, Carlos? And how you cried, having fallen, when you least wanted to, in love with a woman, already, as far as you were concerned, dead.

I am a Pisces. And I think it is not yet fall.

For months you cried.

And tied me to the bed.

And fucked me in every broken-down villa.

And lit candles. And prayed to Saint Jude. Despite what Ana Julia said.

And played a blue guitar. You played a mournful and a blue guitar.

I called you superstitious and vain. I called you terrible names.

Because all along I have just wanted to live.

He dressed me in leather. He made a leather gag.

And blindfold. In every falling-down villa. And we were alive.

I want you never to die, Ava Klein.

He puts his finger in the palm of my hand.

I always knew I'd see you again. We danced to Prince in the circular room. I was quite burned by the sun.

We were working on an erotic song cycle. It was called *A Thousand and One Nights*.

Gently now.

Let's stay in the gardens until evening.

Watering the roses.

There is no plan, no blueprint, and we have to rely on the information of local kids who used to play Hide and Seek in here, Tomás writes.

I looked up and you were gone.

No more second chances.

Max Frisch on Ingeborg Bachmann in his beautiful book *Montauk*. Because I am not, I can see now, going to get there in time:

I think of Ingeborg and her attitude toward money. A handful of banknotes, a FEE, made her as happy as a child, and then she would ask me what I wanted. Money was there to be used. And the way she spent it—not as a reward for work done, but as something from the privy purse of a duchess, if often an impoverished one. She was used to doing without things—money was just a matter of luck. Her money, my money, our money? One either had it or one hadn't and when it didn't stretch she was amazed, as if the world had lost its sense. But she never complained. She did not even notice that radio stations, which were always after her, paid her much too little, and with an air of absent-mindedness she would sign publishing contracts that did the publishers little honor. She never calculated on others' being calculating. She bought shoes as if for a millipede. I don't know how she did it. I cannot remember her ever regretting money spent: a high rent, a handbag from Paris which was ruined on the beach. Money vanishes whatever you do. If somebody whom she loved economized on himself, she considered that a slight to their love. Both of us really deserved a palace, large or small, but she was not indignant because it was somebody else who had it. To give her presents was a joy: she radiated pleasure. She did not demand luxury, but when it was there she was equal to it. Her family background was lower-middle-class like my own, but she had liberated herself from it. Not through ideology, but by force of character. When she reckoned up her accounts, she reckoned with miracles. As with many women, the banknotes in her purse were usually crumpled, ready to be mislaid or turned into something nicer. For my fiftieth birthday she invited me to Greece.

I came to praise.

The privilege of your touch. Even for one night once.

A few hours.

Precious. Disappearing things.

Your black hair like music.

I will never see you again.

Because there are hands. And the perfume of this wildly flowering garden, and the smell of evening coming on.

And the sea.

He spoke of Trieste, of Constantinople. He pushed the curls from his face. He was adapting Dante for the screen. He thought of buying a hat, perhaps. It was how the days went—

Sophie and I used to take the rabbit path around the cliff.

So blue, still and calm. . . .

Do you remember the day I threw myself in the Rhône? You fished me out. My clothes dried in the sun.

In handfuls let us scatter violets and white roses.

And I find myself a little shakier than I used to be.

[211]

Vienna la sera, Francesco.

Who is this girl who is so curious? So in love with everything?

Let's stay in the garden then . . . with the cats and the last—you are ravishing.

Sitting in this room with you and feeling—oh, so many things—inevitability, joy.

So no more helmets, please.

No more second opinions. It's OK.

Love, of course. And fear. A certain fear.

Some pain.

I wouldn't call it suffering.

A horse vaccine from China.

With the cat called Mimi so near, nearing the black square of night.

Tell me again, everything you want.

I'm feeling the form—finally.

A more spacious form. After all this time.

Breathe.

I enter mortal time, Danilo. I feel its draw and pull.

You place a clay ring on my finger. I go back to earth soon.

I love you, Ava Klein. I have come many kilometers to tell you this in person.

Sing me a Yiddish song. There's still time.

In opera, no less than in the other arts, the mind needs freedom to roam, uninhibited.

Let me know if you are going to Central Park.

We dine on trays next to the fire. We miss you.

Will night never come?

NIGHT

This is probably the last love letter I will ever write.

Sing me a Yiddish song.

I kiss you.

Sing me a lullaby by Brahms.

You spoke once more of Trieste.

Queen of the Night.

I feel the Birdcatcher is near.

Thunder is heard.

Silver bells—for your protection.

A magic flute.

Sung in German.

I kiss you one hundred times.

On those evenings we saw forever.

The free world.

City of night.

He was always very tender with me.

I will.

A solitary night once.

A country road. A tree. Evening.

Louis and Louise and the giant poodle Lily.

In the winter do the trees still have the sensation of having leaves—though the leaves have fallen?

And I do not want to miss the cold.

Star light, star bright.

First star.

Your heart beating beneath my hand.

Make a wish.

Almost everything is yet to be written by women about their infinite and complex sexuality, their eroticism.

Ravishing, enchanting

Let me know if you are going.

Bearer of every kind of news.

What did she yearn for? What did she want? What were her hopes? Her unattainable goals?

Ninety, ninety-one, ninety-two, ninety-three. . . .

What did she dream?

Who was she?

And where is she going?

How we liked so much to go to the park. Father would do his funny walk. That made us all laugh so hard we fell in the grass. He'd call to me: Sophie, help! his arms outstretched.

Like the room in a dream.

Whisper in my heart. Tell me you are there.

Accuse me again, if you like, of overreaching.

The child learns her alphabet.

The mystery of your touch

Hovering and beautiful alphabet.

Of wanting too much.

After the masked balls, after the jokes—

I make no apologies. . . .

Look for this in my shoe.

Snow falls on Mozart's grave tonight.

It is given. It is taken away.

Feathered and bejeweled, masked, because in Venice in 1632 *the plague is over.*

To be sung.

It is given back. Sometimes, it is given back.

Our passion for pasta, focaccia, and every fish in the sea.

Use a wooden pestle not to crush, but rather to push the ingredients in a circular motion against the stone which will grind them.

Bombs fell.

Children lived there.

Small paper boat.

Bolting between two subway cars in pursuit of a man who has grabbed her purse, she falls and is dragged by the moving train.

Open sea.

Her brother Paul: I do not think she will come here again. But I told my mother we had to go once.

The sound of guns is near.

Just once.

My sister was beautiful, he said. We are Buddhists. We believe that her spirit is alive and will have another life. I hope she will be beautiful again.

A place to collect things I don't want to forget:

Salamander. Praying mantis. Small horse. Star.

The way your hair caught the light.

So much desire.

She watches shooting stars.

Confetti. Quinze août.

Shortened—how can this—

Half-breathed response to your fingers, tongue.

Coming back from the place we've gone.

The tear in the curtain.

Veined ceiling.

Light.

Don't forget.

She screams.

The sea-soaked steps.

The souls being pulled out of the mouths of the dead.

By mistake—

I do not think she will come here again.

4. Sergei Nabokov (1900–1945) had, like his father, a passionate interest in music, especially

As we form our first words

Who knows where love goes?

The last movement begins with—

That night she dreamt of a shining marble city on a hill.

They hid in a red village.

French baby gifts: Salt for wisdom, an egg,

The next day, exploring, she found the cemetery.

Floating world.

La Régence: 18 July

A change in light, a tilt of the head, a repositioning of legs, the introduction of clouds. Fragments of conversation. A shift in intention. The light board. The cars and vans with their fleeting alphabets. Drama of tourists. Daily drama of lovers. Music in the square. . . .

Let me know—

He calls me with clicks and hisses.

Love, the stars are falling all around us.

I still think of you, after all this time.

The heat of July. I shall not forget. And dancing.

You held my hand.

Bernard

I do not think he will come again.

The last movement begins with a slow introduction in F# minor.
There follows an allegro in A major. I intended for the high-
spiritedness of this music to last throughout the movement, but I
found that I was overtaken by sadness in the last few pages, and I let
it stand that way.

Like a miracle in my arms.

I'm right here.

You spoke of Trieste, of Constantinople. You pushed the curls
from your face. You thought of buying a hat, perhaps—it was how
the days went.

I love you. Have always loved you. I have come, Ava Klein, many
kilometers to tell you in person.

Careful of the intercom.

To this beautifully decorated box.

I miss the old days at the Academy—when we were all there
together.

And we sang.

Brightly colored stitched messages. So many names. A quilt too big to display now. A quilt the size of the earth soon.

Green, how much I want you green.

Aldo Santini. Cherished—

Each occasion celebrated with verve.

Find a cure.

Well, auf Wiedersehen, as he said to me. Too late.

This is probably my last love letter

Find a cure.

But I remember, don't you, what it was like?

Find a cure.

How soon we become bright colors and stitches.

A few threads.

I will never see you again.

Find a cure.

One last glimpse. . . .

Well, auf Wiedersehen, as he said

His footprint in the ice.

Let me know if you are going. The nurses at their stations.

Central Park. I walked for a long time, wept bitter tears, brought you back

A ginkgo leaf. You smiled. Pet it with one finger. You had only hours to live then. We remembered the bridge, the color of rocks, the ginkgo trees

Sweet lavender and thyme.

Yes. You were quite burned by the sun.

And in another park: swan boats. Where we sang.

A bowler hat.

Father would do his funny walk

And how my own mother has always seemed a shadow

It was called *Precious Last Glimpses.*

It's getting late.

The touch of the sun

And how dusk and the moment right before the shapes are taken back by the night is erotic.

And the dark.

The look in your face as you turn away

And we follow it into forever, whispering, the too familiar.

The small light a candle can give.

Sitting here and counting the small beads of sweat on your face is erotic, and the way you toss your head, the curve of your shoulder, the circular garden, the late afternoon, and the memory of

And the dark.

We were all a little in love with her.

[222]

The drag and pull of the park.

She showed us how to dance.

The moan of roses.

In a circle holding hands.

I have been terribly lonely here. Not because I have been too much alone but because I simply have not had a kindred spirit (except for an Italian woman, on the train, who lives in Warsaw). It has been a strange experience, really difficult—but it has perhaps led to a kind of "transcendence" because my friends, amité, has taken on such great value for me. I could almost grow teary-eyed simply writing the word.

I miss you.

The bread in braids.

Why did I think I would give in so gently?

Why did I imagine gentleness?

We used to take the rabbit path around the cliff.

And I find myself a little shakier than I used to be.

Ramon Fernandez, tell me, if you know
Why when the singing ended and we turned
Toward the town,

I know this letter will probably never get to you. But it is important and so I write it anyway.

How, then, to find the arabesque? The dancers?

A million swallows at sunset. Let's get lost in the pattern of rugs. A citadel. A minaret. The gate leading to the mosque. Open me.

How is this for an ending?

Artist's statement: I certainly admire many narrative and documentary films, but instead of re-creating or reproducing a familiar world it's been more exciting to collect an odd assortment of images, both scripted and shot from real life,

Today you could step off the end of the world and float.

And in Czechoslovakia she said: Black sunflower field

You were a boy like any other

He grew roses.

In my memory the white flower seems always to be in blossom.

There were swans there.

She wore blue shoes.

Danilo reads me a letter from his father far away.

Ready or not.

Siebenundneunzig, achtundneunzig, neunundneunzig, hundert.

. . . like the sweet apple
that has reddened
at the top of the tree,
at the top of the topmost bough,
and the apple-pickers
missed it there—no, not missed, so much
as could not touch . . .

What I mean by this, Danilo, is that I think *Aquarium* and *Broken Sky* are beautiful books that mean a lot to me. I am very proud of you, my son. I'm sorry that I never said so: when you were right here.

We were working on an erotic song cycle. It was called *At the Border of Silence.*

It was called *Resonances of the Night.*

We were working on an erotic song cycle. It was called *On the Verge of Disappearing.*

It was called *Like the Sweet Apple That Has Reddened.*

Danilo—

What is it, Ava Klein?

Tell them that you saw me—that it wasn't far—from here to the nurses' station and back,

But that you saw me

And that I flew.

Somewhere snow falls.

And the drowned man says:
Together with me recall: the sky of Paris, that giant autumn crocus. . . .
We went shopping for hearts at the flower girl's booth:
they were blue and they opened up in water.

He is making a film now called *The War Requiem.* He sends me a helmet.

We could go for a song.

He drags pails of sand

It was called *The Darkest Evening of the Year.*

It was called *In the Land of Sand and Ashes.*

Her life for a song.

It's a mirage.

Everything has been taken care of.

Slower now.

This won't hurt so much.

Breathe in. Breathe out.

Such clarity finally. Why not earlier? Why at such cost?

That's an almond tree. There a cherry. Small fig.

Ash.

Not to worry.

Today Danilo says he felt the form of his new book and the form did not betray him but set him free.

He gave her an aquarium. He filled it with small black fish. She said, Don't they look exactly like music?

Begin the story there this time.

Soft music. A nocturne, perhaps.

How was it I thought that in the end it would be easy?

In the Country of Last Hopes.

Could ever be easy?

A festival of lights on the year's darkest night.

Four dolphins. Five-Star Metaxa.

Twelve fish.

Green, how much I want you green. Green wind and green branches.

Your mood changes, Carlos, and in a moment what was sunny and bright and endless days without worry or care is suddenly black, fearsome, irrevocable night.

The tide goes out.

Snow on water.

I am a Pisces, after all.

One does not really feel the need so much to sum up.

We are already in autumn. And the sea is only three and a half miles away.

Now, as you leave the room, with sudden misgivings and in pain.

Some pain.

I go there and find that astonishing brightness in the heart of darkness. Julian coming in with his French lesson; Angelica hung with beads, riding on Roger's foot; Clive claret-colored and yellow like a canary—

I think it is the happiest thing on earth.

Spaghetti poured into a colander.

Darling Francesco.

Because we always knew, didn't we, that at any moment our luck might be up?

Dark hair. Deep sea green eyes.

Let us celebrate, while youth lingers, and ideas flow

And the seduction that is, that has always been language.

Su Friedrich: The challenge comes in trying to push film beyond its usual narrative capacities—so that the form takes as many risks as the content.

Leonard storing apples above my head. And the sun coming through a pearly glass shade; so that the apples which still hang are polish red and green; the church tower a silver extinguisher rising through the trees. Will this recall anything? I am so anxious to keep every scrap, you see.

It's Tuesday. Edith Piaf is singing. It always reminds me of you—

Every moment has been a moment of grace.

To walk on this earth with you. To hold your hand.

The lemons on those trees lit the night.

One hundred shining love letters.

For all of Hesse's determined testing and experimentation with materials, she knew latex was not a permanent substance. *Sans I, Sans III* and *Stratum* have, at this writing less than seven years later, already disintegrated. Other latex pieces, unless they have been kept away from light and heat, have lost the original syrupy surface and color modulations and have darkened to a deep brown; eventually they too will dry up, crack and collapse into dust, unless some sort of fixative substance is discovered quickly.

The ultimate trust—to let go in the dark.

Ravishing, feminine night.

I do not really believe I will be asked to leave.

For one moment she glimpses V.

On the square smaller and smaller dogs.

I heard a fly buzz

Everything smaller

She writes V. Quiet. Listen.

Because it ends.

Tell him that you saw us.

The lovely V at the end of the alphabet.

I was wholly successful in that quest, finding all I wanted on a steep slope high above Telluride—quite an enchanted slope, in fact, with hummingbirds and humming moths visiting the tall green gentians that grew among the clumps of a blue lupine, *Lupinus parviflorus*, which proved to be the food plant of my butterfly.

Hovering and beautiful alphabet—

As we struggle to make meaning,

Where maybe there is none.

And so one let it all go.

We dine on trays, next to the fire, and think of you.

Give everything up, you said. I know a place we can still go.

The boys you arranged for me. The boys you watched me with

Because it ends, is ending.

Under the pomegranate tree in spring.

We took the overnight train. . . .

Beautiful passing landscape. Imagined in the dark.

You kissed me everywhere.

Tell me everything you want.

Close up you are like a statue

The whole world opening and closing.

The unexplored coasts of her body—though it did not seem possible.

And opening

Never stop.

Close up you are like a statue, I whisper, lying on top of him. My fingers in his ringletted hair.

In the night—

I saw you. It looked like you. I saw you in the distance in front of the wall.

You wore a dark star.

Don't forget to make holes for the air.

We laughed so hard we fell in the grass.

So many things, he told me, can attack the rose.

The light in your eyes.

She used a coconut shell.

June was always rainy there.

He gave me a penny for every shiny Japanese beetle I could collect in a glass jar with a lid. We'll have to make holes..

Far away a war on.

Oh I try to imagine how one's killed by a bomb. I've got it fairly vivid—the sensation: but can't see anything but suffocating nonentity following after. I shall think—oh I wanted another 10 years—not this—

Not this.

Alba, Gallica, Damask, Centifola. Cuisse de Nymphe Emue. Such beautiful roses.

Children lived there.

Like his father, he grew old roses.

She sang like a bird.

Sing me a song by Brahms.

She wore a yellow star.

What might have been—

Not this.

And she was beautiful.

The hypnotic room. At the top of the stairs. A far-off green light in the night.

At the lip of the sea. On Christmas Eve.

How can you ask me to go there without

She shines in the grocery shop with a candlelit radiance stalking on legs like beech trees, pink glowing, grape clustered pearl hung.

Almost everything is yet to be written by women—

I miss you.

I'm afraid my fractured wrist is healing very slowly. I am still very much a one-armed girl. Just keeping enough strength to hug you when you arrive.

Come quickly!

I miss the part that never loved you.

Never got to love you.

You wore black taffeta and sang.

You were ravishing.

I miss you.

Sleep,

Ingeborg Bachmann.

Many kinds of love were possible.

Let the record show.

When we are gone

Those who love war, Natalie Barney wrote, lack the love of an appropriate sport—the art of living.

And Natalie Barney knows.

Many kinds of love.

It is the best side of myself. This is what finally counts, independently of any recognition, awards and honors: the extent to which this relationship, despite whatever disabilities or omissions, represents an honest effort to transcribe an intellectual journey. This is what remains in the end. This is why inventory is taken.

Francesco comes in carrying a large wooden crate. Le Beaujolais Nouveau est arrivé, he bellows.

I cannot imagine surviving anymore. When you find my body,

A wild rose.

Dancing at the seaside resort—off-season.

Little seaside star

In my feather and bejeweled mask.

He assembles the trapeze. The waterwheels.

I think she's going a little mad.

And off-screen now—Francesco weeping.

People express their love and affection. Worry and concern.

But you can't blame her.

People prepare what they have wanted to say.

I know this letter will probably never get to you. But it is important
so I write it anyway

Odd conversations, bits of dialogue, letters, and now and then, the
things that mattered most.

They used to go to the river. She brought plantains and fish. She
sang him a cradle song.

We waited for God's word, in vain.

I remember when it was still called Ceylon.

Even you've come!

The first time I swam across the lake you followed in a boat.

We walked in the Beech Forest. We imagined the birds from their
songs.

The small light the candle gave and how your face flushed.

[233]

Is there salvation for you when a film is finished?

He carries an iris. She cradles a blue moon.

Do you remember me?

Yes, but only vaguely. No, I suppose not really.

The labyrinth of Crete, the mystery of water, home.

Careful, he might see you.

You are dreaming.

A change of season.

What a beautiful autumn you must be having there!

Remember the ocean now, Ava.

She puts a cool cloth on my head.

If there was a clearing in that woods, Ava, my mother whispers, I
never saw it.

I'm sorry. I think I must have hurt you very badly. I had your child.
Yes, after just one night. She was called Sophie.

You are dreaming, Ava Klein.

Sophie?

You are dreaming.

First star.

They took the park away. They took away his funny hat. The apples,
the bread.

Yes, Sophie.

The way he walked.

Anais in love with this last dating-service date. Thank you, Ava Klein, for some great answers. Thank you for everything.

He loved roses.

And we would fall in the grass.

Mold a mound at the bottom of each hole to serve as a kind of pillow, set the bud union on top of the soil cushion and spread the roots down the sides.

Bury it two inches under the surface to protect it from winter

I know a place we can still go.

Regard the rose—a cane in the air—shorn of its burden of metaphor.

The buds redden and swell, after days.

Green leaves.

They make a noise like wings.

Alba, how much I love you, Alba.

It was around this time he stopped painting definite things.

Turn over on your side, Ava Klein.

A throbbing. A certain pulsing.

We walked in the Black Forest. I vowed to live,

It was,

Yes, it was, certainly

It was beautiful there.

We sang *Dido and Aeneas*.

I am tired of overwriting, probably. A book of short stories, two "novels," a play in under two years. They go out into the usual void and I hear little more about them.

I remember that remote chorus. My life was music and boys singing so sweetly. We walked to Lincoln Center together holding hands. I to my coach and you off for an afternoon with Philip and Rachel. One of the thousands of afternoons that were ours. It was everything, Ava. I have not forgotten.

Those magic and ordinary afternoons with you.

We had prolonged the world, a little while at least, with song.

You became renowned. You traveled far. I missed you,

Aldo.

Sing to me of last things,

A capella. A capella, now,

I am losing the vague dread.

Wanting everyone and everything.

Prolonging the world with song.

This is Anatole, my new husband, I said to you in Paris when you passed through that fall.

And always such good taste, Ava Klein, you smiled.

I have come to Venice to celebrate. Because *the plague is over!*

She danced. She laughed. She was happy to be here.

So no more chemotherapy, OK? No more wigs. No nausea. Not now.

And absolutely no bone marrow transplants.

It was pleasure to talk as we did

Morning sickness. Mother and Emma brought you sweet drinks and held your hand. Everything about you scared me then. Your swollen breasts and belly.

If you had only one wish—

We lost the baby, Anatole.

Courage.

One hundred more days.

They whisper Tourrettes like the indecipherable word in a dream.

Something half-heard. Just out of the ear's reach.

Glass flowers.

A great deal of Márquez's book therefore is construable as post-humous present with the constant implication that insatiable as it is, the obsessing eye takes in the merest fraction of available phenomena and has to make do with, in fact, next to nothing.

Presque.

Tourrettes-sur-Loup:

Better to see it this way at first. In the rain, a place I had once loved, as much as I had loved anything—a place I had been away from a long time. Away from this place I had grown old. Or if not quite old then older: serious illness or mental collapse had intervened. Rare blood disease. Coming back I felt recovered. I was back in that time before it had occurred. All the faces in the café come back. Behind the bar they all resume their past positions. They remember me and do not. I remember them and do not. I could tap them on the shoulder. I almost died, I might say. It was terrible. I wasn't allowed to travel to you. I can't tell you how much I've missed it here. This altogether unexceptional village in France. You all meant the world to me. And now how strange—

The leaves fall early this autumn, in wind

Francesco, what are you doing here?

They are growing old here. And the young, not quite so young. All the boys I made love to. What could they have thought of me? This Américaine wanting everyone and everything.

Rain. Pas de soleil. And yes it is a little cold today. Vraiment l'hiver, the women say.

And I see him again—though I have not thought of him in many years. He is older now, and more spectacular somehow, by the fountain. Could he, I wonder, for any more than just one dizzying summer, long ago now, have been mine?

She is sheltered by a broken umbrella, still alive.

I have come back whole, Anatole. Hold me close.

If not here, then where?

Bone marrow transplant. One late last hope.

Radio Thin Air.

A teeny, tiny television

A little tree in a dish.

Don't give up, the nurses whisper.

I have not gone back since that night. I remember the sobs. The plastic body bag.

The remote chorus of boys.

[238]

The *Wanderer* Symphony.

He came from out of nowhere, we were having cocktails outside
with the women. You were quite burned by the sun. His name was
Jean-Luc or something like that. He thought you were beautiful.
You were wearing a white dress without straps. You smelled of
lotions. We were cooking a French fish we did not know the name
of. I remember its tail, the shape of its tail, on the plate. Anatole was
already dead.

Hand me that helmet.

Odd how the cuckoo in France sounds just like the clock.

Every day tea, and at the same time.

Teatime. Every day.

And on the phonograph, Mozart.

And the nightingale.

I miss you both more than I can say.

We dine on trays and wait for you.

Do take care.

And maybe it was the love of women I wanted all along—

That either of you should ever be hurt.

Best love,

How could I have hesitated?

A man I did not know put his hand on my leg—

And what in all of it exhausted you?

The harshness of the sun? The admittedly superficial conversation, the games of Pony and Song and Innuendo and Despair? And all so very French. When he appeared out of nowhere you went off together, you said, to dance. You lacked discretion, the French couple said.

He places a tablet on my tongue.

Count the almonds. Do not be afraid anymore.

Seventy-eight, seventy-nine, eighty, eighty-one . . .

Always we just wanted the same thing.

All along and always

Late August thunder.

And you can't imagine what it's like to see your father in a strait-jacket.

We were a peace-loving people.

The day will finally come

Blood and seawater have identical levels

The day will finally come, wrote Marie Leneru in 1915, when our duty will no longer be to accept war and be quiet, but to judge and revolt.

What is this?

A few Chinese herbs. Open your mouth, now.

The same corner you once turned in bright light, in ultraviolet light—

We only had one chance at all this—I believe that.

Three more tablets now. Chinese herbs.

Swallow now. I might have gone to China. They might have been named Shi Sun, Victor Chang, Steve Ning.

An unlikely and beautiful chorus of boys

The leaves fall early this autumn, in wind.
The paired butterflies are already yellow with August,
Over the grass in the West garden;
They hurt me. I grow older.
If you are coming down the narrows of the river Kiang,
Please let me know beforehand,
And I will come out to meet you
                As far as Cho-fu-Sa.

One by one now: an almond tablet, a chrysanthemum tablet, zinnia, in the garden after dark.

They might have been my friends.

It should always be this way—

Let us sit in the garden now and chew with pointy teeth, chrysanthemum tablets.

I will come out to meet you.

Baskets of fruit, jeweled fish on a tray, he falls on his knees, he says *live.*

God bless Mamma and Papa, Ava, Angelina, Maria Regina, Uncle Giuseppe, Jesus your son, Mary the Immaculate Virgin, and Anna Magnani, amen.

Everything in me is suddenly beginning to emerge clearly. Why not earlier? Why at such cost? I have so many thousands of things, some new, some from an earlier time, which I would like to tell you.

I wanted you to be the Queen. I wanted to give you

Putti and the earth's fruit in golden stone against dark trees.

God bless you.

And how we wept through Venice, the water city. You leave me again or I leave you, only this time for good.

Marry me once more, Ava Klein.

Who is that woman dressed in silks and laden with flowers you go with this time?

Why not earlier? Why at such a cost?

I have a great desire to get on with my work but can't get near it at the moment. I see a little clearly at last what my writing is about and fear I have about ten years' courage and energy to get the job done. The feeling of getting oneself in perfection is a strange one, after so many years of expression in blindness.

It's not over quite yet, I whisper.

Don't look so sad.

Marry me—

Fractured with sadness.

What was it I could not ask of you, and therefore never get?

It's only thunder.

One thousand Chinese murdered in a square.

He empties bags of sand into this last room.

Tell me if you are going.

Who besides you?

If not you, Francesco, then who? To take my hand. To say no more now. To pull the infamous plug, if necessary?

Danilo!

And it occurs to me

We were a peace-loving people. Despite the evidence.

It's taken all this time

And it occurs to me now, Francesco

Conrad's *Heart of Darkness* is still a fine story but its faults show
now. The language is too inflated for the situation. Kurtz never
comes to life.

A row of dark trees.

Beyond the Jade Pass, the road is far,
Few couriers come from Chin-ling.
Alone I shed a thousand lines of tears,
When I opened your letter from thousands of miles away.

This is probably the last time I will write you.

Faces in the mirror.

His know-it-all face. His face of desire. His clown face. La Joconde
face. The face of I am sorry

Sorry and we were

And it occurs to me now, Francesco

He bounded up the sea-soaked steps, carrying oysters, clams, sea
urchins, crayfish, mussels, lobster. The fruits of the sea, he said in
English. The jewels of the sea, and laid them at my feet. Twelve fish.
It was Christmas Eve day. That night we ate twelve fish. The green
light of the lighthouse, snow on the beach. He knelt at my feet. One
wave after the next over me. The sound of the foghorn. The smell of
the sea. And sex. Will you marry me? Will you marry me? Will you
marry me?

I will.

What is it that I wanted?

And it occurs to me now, Francesco. After the masked balls after the jokes—

We needed more time and everything in the world.

We were working on an erotic song cycle. It was called *Duet for the End of the World*.

Let's sit in the garden with Anna Magnani for awhile

There's still time.

Compositions of water and sand, fleeting, but sharp and definite for their moment of coherence.

When they speak of the blue fin, the yellow tail, the great red, the fishermen's eyes haze over seeing something far off

Glistening

Why save your songs for spring?

Almost everything is yet to be written—

After the courtyards and palm trees, after the arches and the spiral staircases, and open doors

Thunder and the dogs.

I am afraid of the desert, have always been afraid.

The president draws a line in the sand.

He cries at a simple game of Hide and Seek.

Known for its mirages and without dunes.

Un, deux, trois. . . .

Count the almonds.

Count all the almonds now.

Jeux d'enfants

Ladybug,

Sing to me of lost things—

Did I ever tell you how my hand trembled the first time I fed a horse? He ate the apple up whole from my palm. And how your father—

Thunder still scares me.

I'm right here.

I went to the left and she went to the right. I was young and she was no longer young then.

Father and Sophie and Sol up a little bit ahead. Mother and I behind.

Fifty feet high. Piles of hair.

Nothing but women's hair

At fifteen pennies a kilo—it was used for cloth.

With the bones—

Fertilizer—at least that's what they tried

Fingerprints on the bannister—

When you find this—

All that was left was his footprint in ice.

Glistening

We picnicked up in the gray hills. Lavender and oregano between the rocks. Someone brought a camera.

Marie-Claude,

It was you. Smile. It occurs to her—

And she says, Children are not enough after all; one wants something to be made out of oneself alone.

She holds a playing card.

Smile. Try to smile now.

And in the piazza—

Our life then: assistants, pretty girls, the paparazzi.

Across the room at a party I see you

You surprise even yourself sometimes, Ava Klein.

Across the room I see

Hurry here.

I am sorry to go on pestering you with all these last-minute thoughts. Postscripts. Post-postscripts.

And didn't we always know that at any minute our luck might be up?

The smell of the breeze. And the sea.

You were all I ever wanted.

Carrying bag after bag of sand

Three scorpions.

A penny apiece.

I looked left and she was gone

Wednesday, September 25th, 1940

All day—Monday—in London; in the flat; dark; carpets nailed to windows; ceilings down in patches; heaps of grey dust and china under kitchen table; back rooms untouched. A lovely September day—tender—three days of tender weather—John came. We are moved to Letchworth. The Garden City was moving us that day. . . . The bomb in Brunswick Square exploded. I was in the baker's. Comforted the agitated worn women.

Nothing but heart and bone.

She was up ahead holding Sol's hand.

Es war Erde in ihnen, und
Sie gruben.

When we would go to the park he would do his funny Charlie Chaplin walk that made us laugh so hard we would fall in the grass.

Small birds on the roof.

That's a phonograph. She and Sophie loved to sing once.

Two young girls picking crocuses, and the light.

How is that then for a beginning?

No. I can't begin again.

You loved to sing once.

Ladybug, ladybug, fly away.
Your house is on fire, and your children have gone away.

Make a wish.

Green, how I need you now, green.
Green the breeze. The branches green.
The small boat far on the sea.

It will never again be the world that it was.

Watering and watering the gardens.

But I remember, don't you, what it was like?

And I am homesick now.

At the edge of the bed.

The free world.

Find a cure.

The world where everything seemed possible.

Dear Francesco,

Much is expressed in the interval. Do not worry so much about our silences when they come. I hear you even then.

Let's travel. I know a place we can still go.

A baptism in the night.

You kissed me everywhere—

And we danced.

Huddled around the fire of the alphabet.

He invented inventions. Swam in the river. Kissed the back of his hand and dreamt of girls.

The tanks had not yet come.

The mystery of your touch.

How we got from there to here

I wish very much we could talk alone.

Every moment was a gift, a blessing.

The fertile delta

You are ravishing.

I love the birds.

We were working on the end. It was called At the Café de la Paix.

Danilo's wish: to put back together somehow, all that was divided.
A beautiful wish, after all.

July. Life and motion. I've never seen you look more beautiful.

One afternoon in an apartment vestibule. You held me up against
the door, lifted my dress a little, whispered, Careful of the intercom.

The pleasure of your touch.

The sound of guns is near.

Those who wore white the day of the bomb were saved.

Girl shot, three.

Oh you're right, I'm sorry, of course, how silly of me. You think
then this is not my best book.

Was not Danilo's reaction, but fury.

Baghdad in flames.

The only so-called civilized country besides South Africa without
national health insurance.

We Americans have forgotten how to be Americans, he says.

Yes, I will. I do. I kiss you one thousand times.

Such beautiful trees.

Shall we take the upper or the lower corniche?

The ideal, or the dream, would be to arrive at a language that heals as much as it separates. Could one imagine a language sufficiently transparent, sufficiently supple, intense, faithful so that there would be reparation and not only separation?

Thank you.

Now, pains in joints, weakness. Pain. Some pain.

Find a cure.

We were working on an erotic song cycle. It was called *Preparations for Nuptials on the Other Side of the Abyss*.

I brought you ginkgo leaves from the path.

You had never seen anything so beautiful and said so—Aldo

And we wept. Just once more I'd like to see your face. Hear you sing—

Now the fear is

I'm thirsty, you said.

Open your hand.

A shiny green beetle inside.

That world all but gone.

Homesick.

The sea in our veins.

At the edge of the bed

The shortest evening of the year.

Waiting on a foreign coast. My body an unfamiliar coast, a foreign coast.

I feel you in me

Still. Tell me again how you would like it.

He hands me the half shell. He hands me the comb. Even the shell sheds tears, he says.

Trust your body now—

Blue shoes that flew.

It's taken all this time

Don't stop

In 1600 Iroquois women organized a "Lysistrata" action, refusing sex or childbearing until unregulated warfare stopped.

Small earth in its blanket of blue.

Broken sky.

I love you.

Flowers in danger

Zinnias are always nice

Love in the hallucinatory afternoon.

A helmet.

Ocean of blood.

If you had one wish

The women cry out and run

Aunt Sophie. You're back! And in a wig!

We never found your body.

She nods. It's all right.

What is it? Say the words out loud

I'm thirsty, she says.

Blow out the candles now.

Pisces (Feb 19–March 20)
A time to move on. Have no doubts or regrets. You are doing the
right thing.

Open your hand.

We do not know her first name or the date of her birth.

Slower now. Gently, at first. In this last room.

Almost everything is yet to be written by women about their infinite
and complex sexuality, their eroticism.

I see you from across the room at a party, and am startled to
realize—

Slowly, now.

Have you left the key in its old hiding spot?

Somewhere snow falls. . . .

Without music, as the piece has been choreographed.

[252]

Su Friedrich: Despite my abiding interest in extending the language of film, I find that people tend to pay more attention to the content—perhaps out of a longstanding, misguided notion that women, unlike men, are more concerned with content than with form.

Tears of joy. Unutterable pleasure. And calm.

In Nigeria, in 1929, tens of thousands of Ebo women marked in symbolic war dress, but without weapons, danced, sang, sat on offending men, freed prisoners, cut telephone wires, set up markets—

Pray for peace.

We were shell-shocked, maimed, wounded by war.

I am standing on a hill looking at Prague again.

At the Children's Museum next to the Jewish cemetery—

Pray for peace.

There were swans there.

We were working on an erotic song cycle. It was called *Landscape with Two Graves*.

Primo Levi stands at the top of the dark staircase.

I can't believe your wings!

The women cry out and run towards the young men, arms laden with flowers which they offer them, saying, Let all this have a meaning. Some of the women pulling quantities of heads off the flowers arranged in armfuls, throw them in their faces. The men shake their hair and laugh, moving away from the women and coming nearer again. Some run away and let themselves fall down limply, eyes closed, hands outstretched. Others are completely hidden by the heaps of flowers the women have thrown over them. There are roses tulips peonies lupins poppies snapdragons asters cornflowers irises euphorbias buttercups campanulas.

You remind me of a little girl I once watched.

This is the way to go.

The poet writes: love. The poet writes: death.

It's taken all this time to be free.

Do you remember the day I threw myself in the Rhône? You fished me out.

My clothes dried in the sun.

Body oils leave the fabric. Sperm and sweat and perfume make a pretty pattern in the water. Like a fingerprint. Carried over the rocks. Good-bye—

I can't believe

It's you, I can't believe it's really you.

The little girl draws the letter A.

Each Independence Day.

The women say,

Merci, mille fois. I kiss you one thousand times.

Rock me to sleep, beautiful Marie-Claude and Emma, by the sea.

How can you ask me to leave?

Everything I ever wanted was there.

On the phonograph

Mozart.

The child contemplates the number 7.

[254]

The glitter of the sea.

Schubert. Brahms.

Good-bye, then.

We do not know her first name, or the year of her birth, only that in 1810 she wrote a sonata

And it is beautiful.

They say how pleasing to them is their contact, how their limbs relax and soften, how their muscles—touched by pleasure—become supple and light, how in this wretched state, when they are marked for death, their bodies—unbound and full of calm—begin to float, how the warm water, pleasing to the touch, carries them to a beach of fine sand, where they fall asleep from fatigue.

So that the form takes as many risks as the content—

It's taken so long to get here.

When I swam across the lake for the first time.

Make a wish.

Let's stay in the garden until dark. The air was pure. The faint smell of bitter herbs.

I was propelled by dreams. Danced. Made love under every sun and the stars

I kiss you,

On the lips,

In the pearly sea light, good-bye.

The rose called Cuisse de Nymphe Emue.

The pink and golden rose called Peace.

1 November
Today is of course a holiday in Europe.

Swallow now.

How did we live then? Do you remember? Did we thank God for the bread we ate? Did we sing Yiddish songs?

Fleeting landscape. Imagined in the dark.

I collected beetles, stones, flowers in a basket. I observed the praying mantis. I blew the wings of the ladybug. All this—

I would carry a glowing basket of oranges across the village.

In the square now, smaller and smaller—

Odd the way my hair is growing in finally, and lighter than it was—as when I was a child.

I made a May basket covered with moss. I made perfume from roses. I cried when you cried.

The girl draws a V from the other side of the alphabet.

This beautifully decorated box.

You were our light in the dark.

In the beloved city of P where we wept, told stories, sang songs, feared death.

In the room under the house my father had a printing press. Made black books fastened with nails. Above ground my mother hung wash. Listened to the radio.

Careful.

I was only a child then, went to school, played in the dusty field, trapped animals, let them go, shelled peas for Mother, felt the fear of the women.

[256]

Rode a small horse.

Collected rocks. Invented inventions. Dreamt of girls.

Breathe. It is given.

Black sunflower field. Small horse. I kiss you, city of P.

Let us celebrate.

Someone has brought black fish—beautiful silent music

Chrysanthemums.

In the night—sirens and lights.

Hold me together with nails and tears.

But when the horse chestnuts are in bloom—

We used to take the rabbit path. . . .

Mother, speak to me just once.

Come quickly, Ava. There are finches at the feeder.

And the drowned man says:
Your hand full of hours, you came to me—and I said:
Your hair is not brown.
So you lifted it lightly on to the scales of grief; it weighed more
than I . . .

A pregnant woman is weeping. She is my sister.

We'll have to hide.

She scribbles a last word

There was earth inside them,
and they dug.

Children lived there.

She sits at the edge of the bed

Her voice, the free world.

And I am pulled toward the irresistible music of the end

And the silence which is

Undeniably lovely

And your lovely face

Every moment has been a moment of grace—

The light is so bright it almost hurts now. Come quickly.

I offer you this.

A moon. Two stars.

What did you fear?

What did you want?

What made you laugh once?

Who were you?

She loved finches. She fed a horse.

Hovering and beautiful alphabet—

To create a language that heals as much as it separates.

—as we form our first words after making love.

I need days in bed with you like this

I'll meet you at Quai 3 at eight.

It seems a little too precious, at least from where I stand now. Too right and too beautiful . . . I'd like to do a little more wrong at this point.

He is on the track of Canaan all his life; it is incredible that he should see the land only when on the verge of death. This dying vision of it can only be intended to illustrate how incomplete a moment is human life, incomplete because a life like that can last forever and still be nothing but a moment. Moses fails to enter Canaan not because his life is too short, but because it is a human life.

We are working on an erotic song cycle. It is called *In the Joie de Vivre Room.*

It is beautiful.

The night swallows are swooping and diving.

In the War Theater it is just past midnight. In the Night Theater.

And I thought that human being out there on display digging her grave is my sister. A halo is glowing around her shriveled body.

In the Philippines women stand in front of the tanks.

A sandstorm. A line of men.

The desert on fire. It's a mirage, it's a mirage.

You are dreaming, Ava Klein.

It was early autumn. Unseasonably warm. All the joggers were out. People on benches. In the distance we could hear the sound of water rushing over rocks. Through the trees the yellow of taxi cabs. We brought a picnic. It felt like summer. The ginkgo trees.

Who was she? And what did she want?

Three husbands. Comparative literature. I do not mean to be

summing up.

I have so many things I would like to tell you.

You are a rare bird, Ava Klein.

The lemon trees are planted along the garden walls. By and by they will be covered with rush mats, but the orange trees are left in the open. Hundreds and hundreds of the loveliest fruits are on these trees. They are never trimmed or planted in a bucket as in our country, but stand free and easy in the earth, in a row with their brothers. You can imagine nothing jollier than the sight of such a tree. For a few pennies you can eat as many oranges as you like. They taste very good now, but in March they will taste even better.

Could she, I wonder, for any more than just one moment in a kitchen in Italy, years ago—

What a beautiful autumn you must be having. I would like to be able to walk along and sit with you and say

The other day we went to the seashore and saw fishermen hauling in their nets. The oddest creatures came up—fish, crabs and weird freaks of nature. Among them was the fish which gives anyone who touches it an electric shock.

I always want to be there, especially on days like today.

There is not a week that goes by that I do not think of you—

The sign says: Fresh Cut Flowers.

And the sign says: Don du Sang.

The ultimate trust: to let go in the dark.

Traipsing around the Hôtel de Ville.

Trust your body now, he says, the way you did then,

Under the pomegranate tree.

[260]

Do you remember?

I remember.

He places a little globe around my neck. Charms. Stars. Amulets. Let me know if you are going

A laurel wreath. Ginkgo leaves

In the doomed and cherished city of N, where I lived

I got to dance. I got to sing. I got to kiss you on the cheek.

I got to . . . careful of the intercom.

I'll never forget the way you looked that night from across the room, at a party. And I am shocked to realize there is no one I could ever love more—or want to love me.

I'll never forget the way you looked.

City of N.

Where

After the masked balls, after the jokes, after sex and spaghetti bolognese. After all the mad aristocrats and decaying palazzi, after the silly plot contrivances, after riding you bareback like a horse on the fur rug in Brescia, after all the Via Venetos and gossip, after the blonde goddesses, the shopping and flirting, after all the philandering, everyone gone home and the piazza deserted—we stand naked in the eerie glow of the street lamp, in front of what seems a slowed-up or backwards-flowing fountain, and say our good-byes—this, Francesco, is how I would like it.

Ramon Fernandez, tell me, if you know—

Women have not made discoveries, because they have been kept from the scene—absolutely. They have been kept from making discoveries.

So much left

This is probably the last time I will write you

Brilliant and broken city of N.

I sent you a million love letters. You probably never got them all.

I sent you an olive branch in the mail.

Traditional French baby gifts: salt for wisdom, an egg for fecundity, bread for goodness and a matchstick.

Without music—

As the piece has been choreographed.

He holds a butterfly net.

How could I have

Open your mouth. Swallow.

One night only, once—

It was called *In the Garden Near Shanghai After Dark*.

Once, long ago,

When you were thinking of making love to me before—how were we doing it

Don't leave anything out.

And what was the light like?

You took the silk scarf from my neck.

You spoke of Trieste,

Against a pulsing field of extraordinary music.

As we form our first words. Flowers in the dark.

We dressed as owls and the sky. I wore the zodiac on my back.

Passing alphabet of the night

Give me your arm. This shouldn't hurt that much—

Breathe.

Sing to me of lost things:

One feels the need in the end for hundreds of daughters:

She is standing at the ditch when all of a sudden she notices a little house off to the right. It is covered with snow and no smoke is coming from the chimney. Ava is next to Sophie and Rachel is next to Ava. The terrible side guards have gone to the rear. In a flash Sophie is running toward the small house. Then Rachel. Then Ava. There is no thinking on their parts. Not a word among them. Just one sister following another.

Sugar
Flour
Eggs
Kosher salt
Honey.

Open your mouth. I promise this won't hurt—

Chrysanthemum, almond tablet

They might have had beautiful, improbable names.

South African women confronting the police fall to their knees and begin to pray.

One sister following another.

Where we could have gone together. And where I can't go alone.

We do not know what she might have been without the men of
Treblinka

Come quickly, Ava.

Blood transfusion.

Even though you were afraid: you held my hand; you said,

Yes, we'll have to make little holes for the air.

Green, how much I want you—green.

Somewhere a young girl learns her alphabet.

My hand reaching for a distant, undiscovered planet.

So much is yet to be written—

Ana Julia Méndez de Herrera: rivers will be named for you.

Why save your songs for spring?

Let's put some roses along the back. The rose called Cuisse de
Nymphe Emue.

Rich they were, rich as a fig broken open, soft as a ripened peach,
freckled as an apricot, coral as a pomegranate, bloomy as a bunch of
grapes.

The rose called Cuisse de Nymphe Emue: Thigh of an Aroused
Nymph,

And how it bloomed once, unreservedly, and not again.

Make a well. Slowly take flour in.

There are so many things I would like—

Ingeborg Bachmann (1926-1973), a major influence on such writers as Günter Grass, Christa Wolf, Max Frisch and Peter Handke. Born in Klagenfurt, Austria. Died in Rome, Italy, from injuries sustained in a fire.

The girl draws an A. She spells her name:

AVA

Today is of course a holiday—

Snow falls like music.

How we celebrated.

One feels the need in the end for hundreds of daughters—

We used to take the rabbit path up and over the hill and we were there.

Come quickly—

You can't believe,

A throbbing. A certain pulsing.

You are ravishing.

ACKNOWLEDGMENTS

With gratitude:

For their practical support: The Michael Karolyi Foundation, The Provincetown Fine Arts Work Center, The Corporation of Yaddo, PEN American Center, Cathy and Jay Giannelli, Lucia Getsi, Judith Karolyi, Zenka Bartek, Helen Lang, and one who wishes to remain anonymous.

For their intelligence: Barbara Page, Barbara Ras, Laura Mullen, and Louis Asekoff—most trusted readers.

For its vision and audacity: Dalkey Archive Press. And to Steve Moore, for his patience without end.

And to the muses—they know who they are—for their perpetual radiance.

SOURCES

What floods the mind of my Ava Klein on her final day include among the many private voices and versions of herself, those voices that arise from her "passionate and promiscuous reading" of the texts of the world. I have attempted as much as possible to attribute the sources of this "irresistible music." When a source is self-evident, I have not cited additional and complicating information here. My hope is that these notes, at some point, will enhance the reader's pleasure but in no way interrupt the trance of the text.

p. 4   "Green, how much I want you green": this is from Federico García Lorca's "Sleepwalking Ballad."

4   "After all the dolci . . . even then?": the rhythms here are Eliot's in "The Love Song of J. Alfred Prufrock."

9   "Tell him that you saw us": from Samuel Beckett's *Waiting for Godot*. Other lines from the play are buried in the novel like treasures.

11   "In an attempt . . . unsuccessful": this refers to the French artist Christian Boltanski (born 1944) and is taken from the introductory catalog essay for his *Lessons of Darkness*.

12   "And in 1971 . . . from sugar cubes": same as above.

13   "He tries to conserve . . . biscuit boxes": again Boltanski.

13   "He makes a record . . . as a child": same as above.

16-17   From an interview with Max Frisch in the *Paris Review*, winter 1989.

20   "The lemon trees . . . with their brothers": this is from Goethe's *Italian Journey*.

21   "A pretty rough show . . . upper body": from Arthur C. Danto's *Encounters and Reflections: Art in the Historical Present*.

22   "The self-portrait . . . a fur boa": same as above.

[269]

22 "With AIDS . . . possible world": the same.

24 "And all the air . . . die yet": from *A Writer's Diary* by Virginia Woolf.

25 "Oh I try to imagine . . . not this": same as above.

33 "When you begin the book": the book in question is Hermann Broch's *Death of Virgil*.

38 "A man in the house . . . your golden hair": this is from Paul Celan's "Death Fugue."

44 "Tyger! Tyger! burning bright": from the poem by William Blake.

45 "And the one-armed man . . . white lily": from Laurie Anderson's *Home of the Brave*.

46 "Ramon Fernandez . . . if you know": from "The Idea of Order at Key West" by Wallace Stevens.

51 "Language for women . . . forms of discourse": this is from *Hélène Cixous: Writing the Feminine* by Verena Andermatt Conley.

61-62 "To Moses . . . true speech": this is from George Steiner's *Real Presences*.

63 "Without inventing . . . any kind": Max Frisch in *Montauk*.

64 "A story . . . is alive": same as above.

73 "When you . . . geography lessons": from Michelangelo Antonioni's *L'Avventura*.

76 "The *Tentation* . . . versions of reality": from Steiner's *Real Presences*.

78 "*Behemoth* . . . long pauses": this refers to choreographer Mark Morris's piece.

79 "A quote from Virginia Woolf": from *A Writer's Diary*.

82 "How often . . . green balcony": from Lorca's "Sleepwalking Ballad."

86 "Artist's statement . . . the image": the artist is Tom Pappas. This was taken from his Fine Arts Work Center opening in 1990.

97 "I am tired . . . more about them": Beckett as quoted in Deirdre

[270]

Bair's biography.

97 "In March . . . her diary": Eva Hesse (1936-1970), quoted in the study by Lucy Lippard.

98 "It is difficult . . . of homelessness": from Steiner's *Real Presences*.

99 "Most of them . . . their purposes": from the film *Shoah* by Claude Lanzman.

99 "Black milk . . . and we": from Celan's "Death Fugue."

100 "You remind me . . . picking flowers": from a fragment by Sappho.

111 "At the gas chamber . . . a nice haircut": from Lanzman's *Shoah.*

113 "You will have . . . The edge": Hélène Cixous, in conversation with Verena Andermatt Conley, January 1982.

117 "They tried . . . the *Hatikvah*": from *Shoah.*

130 "No character . . . decorated box": from Guy Davenport's *Every Force Evolves a Form.*

131 "The only reality . . . is company": same as above.

131 "Whisper . . . you are there": from Goethe's *Italian Journey.*

133 "After a few days . . . regret it": Colette as quoted in her biography by Joanna Richardson.

139 "The writing . . . your life": from Jorge Luis Borges's *Atlas.*

140 "As Gonzalo . . . beautiful books": from Anaïs Nin's *Diary.*

141 "You will use . . . have died": from Borges's *Atlas.*

142 "As I write . . . in Mallorca" / "It could be . . . your paradise" / "It could be . . . the ocean": Borges, same as above.

143 "The women . . . a meaning": from Monique Wittig's *Les Guérillères.*

146 "He wants . . . his life": from Frisch's *Montauk.*

146 "I penetrated . . . platonic sea": from Goethe's *Italian Journey.*

147 "I began . . . to hear 'Volare' ": Herschel Garfein's (born 1958) notes on his String Quartet (1990).

148 "The planet on the table": title of a poem by Wallace Stevens.

151 "There are times . . . so delirious": this is Lorca, from the introduction to his *Collected Poems.*

152 "Late one night . . . decorated box": this is Joseph Cornell's sister Elizabeth speaking of her brother, as recounted in Dore Ashton's *A Joseph Cornell Album.*

158 "Soon it was clear . . . a dark apple": Lorca.

163 "The ideal . . . separation": Cixous in conversation with Conley.

165 "Song of the Unborn Child . . . his little boat": by Lorca.

184 "Shifting voices . . . or analysis": Rosmarie Waldrop on Edmond Jabès in *Epoch.*

185 "Part of me . . . doesn't last": Eva Hesse, from Lippard's book.

187 "I have seen . . . to tell you": from Goethe's *Italian Journey.*

191-92 "It is intellectually . . . feel them": Nadia Boulanger on Bach, from Dan G. Campbell's *Master Teacher: Nadia Boulanger.*

192-93 "Still if he could . . . in the distance": from Woolf's *To the Lighthouse.*

197 "Do you remember . . . dried in the sun": from Beckett's *Godot.*

201 "I go on loving you like water": from John Ashbery's "Tennis Court Oath."

202 "I have a great . . . quite at rest": from Woolf's *A Writer's Diary.*

203-4 "Mr. Angelopoulos . . . Let us say the fall": from an interview that appeared in *Periodiko,* August 1989.

206 "He felt too good . . . never recur": from Frank O'Hara's *Early Writing.*

216 "A country road . . . Evening": stage setting for *Godot.*

216 "Almost everything . . . their eroticism": from Cixous's "The Laugh of the Medusa."

220 "The last movement . . . stand that way": from Garfein's program notes to his String Quartet.

223 "Ramon Fernandez ... toward the town": from Stevens's "Idea of Order."

224 "Artist's statement ... real life": Su Friedrich (born 1954), from a statement accompanying the Whitney Museum's "New American Filmmakers" series in 1987.

224 "like the sweet apple . . . not touch": Sappho.

225 "Together with me ... in water": from Paul Celan's "Memory of France."

227 "I go there . . . like a canary": from Woolf's A *Writer's Diary*.

227 "Let us celebrate ... ideas flow": Ree Morton (1936-1977), from a piece of the same name: paint on canvas, elastic, and wood (1975).

228 "Leonard storing . . . you see": from Woolf's A *Writer's Diary*.

228 "For all of Hesse's ... discovered quickly": from Lippard's *Eva Hesse*.

228 "I heard a fly buzz": from the Emily Dickinson poem.

229 "I was wholly ... my butterfly": a letter from Vladimir Nabokov to Edmund Wilson, in *The Nabokov–Wilson Letters*.

230 "Oh I try . . . not this": Woolf in A *Writer's Diary*.

231 "She shines . . . pearl hung": Woolf on Vita Sackville-West.

241 "The leaves fall ... Cho-fu-Sa": the conclusion to "The River-Merchant's Wife: A Letter" by Li Po, as translated by Ezra Pound.

242 "I have a great desire ... in blindness": this is Beckett as quoted in the biography by Bair.

243 "Beyond the Jade Pass ... miles away": this is a poem I memorized as a little girl and have not been able to find again.

247 "All day . . . worn women": Woolf's A *Writer's Diary*.

247 "Es war . . . gruben": from Paul Celan's poem of the same title.

253 "The women cry ... buttercups campanulas": from Wittig's *Les Guérillères*.

255 "They say . . . from fatigue": same as above.

[273]

257 "Your hand full . . . than I": from Celan's "Your Hand Full of Hours."

257 "There was earth . . . they dug": from the Celan poem of the same title.

259 "It seems . . . at this point": Eva Hesse, as quoted in Lippard's biography.

260 "The lemon trees . . . even better" / "The other day . . . electric shock": this is Goethe in his *Italian Journey*.

264 "Rich they were . . . grapes": Vita Sackville-West in a letter to Virginia Woolf.

DALKEY ARCHIVE PAPERBACKS

FICTION: AMERICAN

BARNES, DJUNA. *Ladies Almanack*	9.95
BARNES, DJUNA. *Ryder*	9.95
BARTH, JOHN. *LETTERS*	14.95
CHARYN, JEROME. *The Tar Baby*	10.95
COOVER, ROBERT. *A Night at the Movies*	9.95
CRAWFORD, STANLEY. *Some Instructions to My Wife*	7.95
DOWELL, COLEMAN. *Too Much Flesh and Jabez*	9.95
DUCORNET, RIKKI. *The Fountains of Neptune*	10.95
DUCORNET, RIKKI. *The Jade Cabinet*	9.95
FAIRBANKS, LAUREN. *Sister Carrie*	10.95
GASS, WILLIAM H. *Willie Masters' Lonesome Wife*	9.95
KURYLUK, EWA. *Century 21*	12.95
MARKSON, DAVID. *Springer's Progress*	9.95
MARKSON, DAVID. *Wittgenstein's Mistress*	9.95
MASO, CAROLE. *AVA*	12.95
McELROY, JOSEPH. *Women and Men*	15.95
MERRILL, JAMES. *The (Diblos) Notebook*	9.95
NOLLEDO, WILFRIDO D. *But for the Lovers*	12.95
SEESE, JUNE AKERS. *Is This What Other Women Feel Too?*	9.95
SEESE, JUNE AKERS. *What Waiting Really Means*	7.95
SORRENTINO, GILBERT. *Aberration of Starlight*	9.95
SORRENTINO, GILBERT. *Imaginative Qualities of Actual Things*	9.95
SORRENTINO, GILBERT. *Splendide-Hôtel*	5.95
SORRENTINO, GILBERT. *Steelwork*	9.95
SORRENTINO, GILBERT. *Under the Shadow*	9.95
STEIN, GERTRUDE. *A Novel of Thank You*	9.95
STEPHENS, MICHAEL. *Season at Coole*	7.95
WOOLF, DOUGLAS. *Wall to Wall*	7.95
YOUNG, MARGUERITE. *Miss MacIntosh, My Darling*	2-vol. set, 30.00
ZUKOFSKY, LOUIS. *Collected Fiction*	9.95

DALKEY ARCHIVE PAPERBACKS

FICTION: BRITISH

BROOKE-ROSE, CHRISTINE. *Amalgamemnon*	9.95
CHARTERIS, HUGO. *The Tide Is Right*	9.95
FIRBANK, RONALD. *Complete Short Stories*	9.95
MOSLEY, NICHOLAS. *Accident*	9.95
MOSLEY, NICHOLAS. *Impossible Object*	9.95
MOSLEY, NICHOLAS. *Judith*	10.95

FICTION: FRENCH

CREVEL, RENÉ. *Putting My Foot in It*	9.95
ERNAUX, ANNIE. *Cleaned Out*	9.95
GRAINVILLE, PATRICK. *The Cave of Heaven*	10.95
NAVARRE, YVES. *Our Share of Time*	9.95
QUENEAU, RAYMOND. *The Last Days*	9.95
QUENEAU, RAYMOND. *Pierrot Mon Ami*	9.95
ROUBAUD, JACQUES. *The Great Fire of London*	12.95
ROUBAUD, JACQUES. *The Plurality of Worlds of Lewis*	9.95
ROUBAUD, JACQUES. *The Princess Hoppy*	9.95
SIMON, CLAUDE. *The Invitation*	9.95

FICTION: IRISH

CUSACK, RALPH. *Cadenza*	7.95
MACLOCHLAINN, ALF. *Out of Focus*	5.95
O'BRIEN, FLANN. *The Dalkey Archive*	9.95
O'BRIEN, FLANN. *The Hard Life*	9.95

FICTION: LATIN AMERICAN and SPANISH

CAMPOS, JULIETA. *The Fear of Losing Eurydice*	8.95
SARDUY, SEVERO. *Cobra* and *Maitreya*	13.95
TUSQUETS, ESTHER. *Stranded*	9.95
VALENZUELA, LUISA. *He Who Searches*	8.00

Dalkey Archive Paperbacks

POETRY

ANSEN, ALAN. *Contact Highs: Selected Poems 1957-1987*	11.95
BURNS, GERALD. *Shorter Poems*	9.95
FAIRBANKS, LAUREN. *Muzzle Thyself*	9.95
GISCOMBE, C. S. *Here*	9.95
MARKSON, DAVID. *Collected Poems*	9.95
THEROUX, ALEXANDER. *The Lollipop Trollops*	10.95

NONFICTION

FORD, FORD MADOX. *The March of Literature*	16.95
GAZARIAN, MARIE-LISE. *Interviews with Latin American Writers*	14.95
GAZARIAN, MARIE-LISE. *Interviews with Spanish Writers*	14.95
GREEN, GEOFFREY, ET AL. *The Vineland Papers*	14.95
MATHEWS, HARRY. *20 Lines a Day*	8.95
ROUDIEZ, LEON S. *French Fiction Revisited*	14.95
SHKLOVSKY, VIKTOR. *Theory of Prose*	14.95
WEST, PAUL. *Words for a Deaf Daughter* and *Gala*	12.95
YOUNG, MARGUERITE. *Angel in the Forest*	13.95

For a complete catalog of our titles, or to order any of these books, write to Dalkey Archive Press, Illinois State University, Campus Box 4241, Normal, IL 61790-4241. One book, 10% off; two books or more, 20% off; add $3.00 postage and handling. Phone orders: (309) 438-7555.